"Okay, it's a deal...."

Ben held out his hand for Clair to shake, and she took it without thinking.

But that perfectly innocent handshake made her extremely aware of the heat of his skin, the strength of his grip, the sensuality of his touch—things she didn't want to be aware of at all. And just the fact that she was, spurred her to say, "I don't think you should walk me to the cottage. I'll just slip out as if I was never here, and we'll be that much closer to putting the reunion behind us and starting over."

"You're sure?"

"Positive." She smiled and left. Somehow she'd gone from nearly hyperventilating at just the thought of seeing Ben Walker again to actually being tempted to linger a while with him. He had an effect on her like no other man ever had.

Although maybe his having unusual effects on her shouldn't have come as such a surprise under the circumstances....

Circumstances in which he'd managed to conquer her infertility!

Dear Reader,

Well, we hope your New Year's resolutions included reading some fabulous new books—because we can provide the reading material! We begin with *Stranded with the Groom* by Christine Rimmer, part of our new MONTANA MAVERICKS: GOLD RUSH GROOMS miniseries. When a staged wedding reenactment turns into the real thing, can the actual honeymoon be far behind? Tune in next month for the next installment in this exciting new continuity.

Victoria Pade concludes her NORTHBRIDGE NUPTIALS miniseries with *Having the Bachelor's Baby,* in which a woman trying to push aside memories of her one night of passion with the town's former bad boy finds herself left with one little reminder of that encounter—she's pregnant with his child. Judy Duarte begins her new miniseries, BAYSIDE BACHELORS, with *Hailey's Hero,* featuring a cautious woman who finds herself losing her heart to a rugged rebel who might break it…. THE HATHAWAYS OF MORGAN CREEK by Patricia Kay continues with *His Best Friend,* in which a woman is torn between two men—the one she really wants, and the one to whom he owes his life. Mary J. Forbes's sophomore Special Edition is *A Father, Again,* featuring a grown-up reunion between a single mother and her teenaged crush. And a disabled child, an exhausted mother and a down-but-not-out rodeo hero all come together in a big way, in Christine Wenger's debut novel, *The Cowboy Way.*

So enjoy, and come back next month for six compelling new novels, from Silhouette Special Edition.

Happy New Year!

Gail Chasan
Senior Editor
Silhouette Special Edition

Please address questions and book requests to:
Silhouette Reader Service
U.S.: 3010 Walden Ave., P.O. Box 1325, Buffalo, NY 14269
Canadian: P.O. Box 609, Fort Erie, Ont. L2A 5X3

Having the Bachelor's Baby

VICTORIA PADE

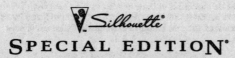

Silhouette

SPECIAL EDITION

Published by Silhouette Books

America's Publisher of Contemporary Romance

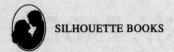

SILHOUETTE BOOKS

ISBN 0-373-24658-7

HAVING THE BACHELOR'S BABY

Copyright © 2005 by Victoria Pade

This edition published by arrangement with Harlequin Books S.A.

Visit Silhouette Books at www.eHarlequin.com

Printed in U.S.A.

Books by Victoria Pade

Silhouette Special Edition

*A Ranching Family
†Baby Times Three
**Northbridge Nuptials

Silhouette Books

World's Most Eligible Bachelors
Wyoming Wrangler

Montana Mavericks:
   Wed in Whitehorn
The Marriage Bargain

The Coltons
From Boss to Bridegroom

Logan's Legacy
For Love and Family

VICTORIA PADE

is a bestselling author of both historical and contemporary romance fiction, and mother of two energetic daughters, Cori and Erin. Although she enjoys her chosen career as a novelist, she occasionally laments that she has never traveled farther from her Colorado home than Disneyland, instead spending all her spare time plugging away at her computer. She takes breaks from writing by indulging in her favorite hobby—eating chocolate.

NORTHBRIDGE NEWS

The bad boy is back...
and better looking than ever!

The one-time bad boy of Northbridge is back in town, but is it for business, as he claims—or for pleasure, as it seems? After taking a quick drive by the old Northbridge School for Boys, the *discreet* reporter noticed just how many changes Ben Walker already made to the place...and how close he seemed to previous owner Clair Cabot. Rumor has it that Ben and Clair got awfully cozy a few months back at the Northbridge High School reunion. And since I'm sworn to report the full story... A source has revealed she recently spotted a trench-coated Clair skimming the titles in Bella's Books— in the childcare section! So how cozy *did* they get that night? Looks like only nine months will tell!

Chapter One

"Northbridge. Thirty miles. Thirty *short* miles..."

Clair Cabot was talking to herself. But reading the sign above the highway out loud as she drove underneath it didn't ease any of the tension she was feeling. In fact, the closer she got to her destination the more her stress level increased.

Northbridge. The small Montana town where fifteen-year-old Clair and her father had moved when her father had purchased a ranch to turn into a school and quasi-boot-camp for troubled preadolescent boys.

The small Montana town where Clair had gone to high school and met and married her high-school sweetheart before moving with him to Denver.

The small Montana town she'd last visited for a single night in June to attend her graduating class's tenth reunion.

The small Montana town where, for the second time in her life, a man had altered her course....

"Take a deep breath and blow it out. Take a deep breath and blow it out," she recited, performing the relaxation technique advised by her doctor when she'd passed out in her office a week ago.

The deep breathing helped a little. Only a little. Because after all, she was still getting closer and closer to Northbridge with every passing minute. To Northbridge and to the Northbridge School for Boys...and to the school's new owner—Ben Walker.

Clair had to do the deep breathing again at just the thought of Ben Walker.

Ben Walker—Northbridge's bad boy.

Or at least that's what he'd been as a teenager. So bad that by the time Clair had arrived in town he'd already been sent to Arizona for a program for adolescents in trouble. Which meant that even though Clair's best friend through high school had been Ben Walker's twin sister, Cassie, Clair hadn't even met Ben until the last semester of senior year when he'd been allowed to come back to graduate with his class. And by then Clair had been so involved with Rob Cabot she hadn't even noticed Cassie's hardtack twin.

Until the reunion in June.

"Stupid reunion," Clair muttered.

But the reunion wasn't to blame for what had happened the last time she was in Northbridge, she thought, contradicting herself. It was Rob Cabot who had set the wheels into motion. It was his fault.

Her ex-husband.

She'd asked him if he was going to the reunion—not face-to-face, she hadn't wanted to *ever* see him again after the divorce. But she'd e-mailed him and asked him.

And that's *all* she'd done—she'd *asked* him. Nicely. Politely. She hadn't goaded him or challenged him or done anything to provoke him. She hadn't even let him know that if he was going, she wasn't—although that had been her plan. She'd only e-mailed and asked him if he was going. A simple question that had only required a simple, straight-forward, *honest* answer.

And that's what she'd thought he'd given her.

He'd said there was no way he was going, that he and his new wife—the woman he'd married less than twenty-four hours after his divorce from Clair had been finalized—had better things to do.

So naturally Clair had figured the coast was clear and she could go. She could go without worrying about seeing Rob. Without worrying about seeing his new wife. Without feeling uncomfortable. Without having to relive the pain of the past eleven months. She could just go and have fun.

Which was all she'd intended to do.

But she should have known better. She should have

known that Rob wouldn't forgo anything so anyone else—especially Clair—could have free rein with it.

So of course, who had she met at the sign-in table within five minutes of arriving at the Northbridge High School gymnasium?

Rob.

And his new wife.

His *pregnant* new wife.

And as if that hadn't been enough salt poured into Clair's wounds, Rob had seized the opportunity to place his hand on his new wife's belly, smile smugly and say, "So now we know *I* wasn't the problem."

The memory of that moment still hurt. It was one of the worst of Clair's life. She'd whispered, "Congratulations," in a shocked, choked voice, and then she'd made a beeline for the ladies room to hide in one of the stalls and sob.

That was where she'd been when her old friend Cassie had found her.

Poor Cassie had spent an hour standing outside the stall door to talk her through her misery until Clair managed to muster enough courage to finally come out.

"I'm going home," she'd announced then.

But Cassie wouldn't hear of it. "I won't let you do that," Cassie had said. "You're here, and you can't just turn around and go back to Denver before we've even had a chance to say hello. It'll be okay. I'll stay right by your side and I won't let Rob get within a hundred yards of you again."

It had taken more talking on Cassie's part to convince Clair, but in the end she'd succumbed and agreed to stay.

But not without a stiff drink.

The problem was, one stiff drink had become two. Then three. Then Clair had lost count.

And although Cassie had tried to be good to her word and remain close by, she'd been the head of the reunion committee and had had other responsibilities and duties that had made that impossible.

Instead, Cassie had sent her twin brother to act as a buffer.

Her twin brother, Ben. Reformed town bad boy. Hunk extraordinaire.

Clair had not minded that Rob had gotten to see her with the best-looking man in the room.

And since one semester at Northbridge High hadn't left Ben a lot of things to reminisce about, once Cassie had turned Clair over to him, Ben had stayed by Clair's side from then on.

Of course even though Clair didn't know it for a fact, she'd assumed that Cassie had told Ben about her situation and, looking back on that night, Clair thought he'd probably just taken pity on her. But it hadn't seemed that way at the time. At the time he'd been disarmingly sweet and charming. His wry observations of their classmates had made her laugh. He'd somehow managed to actually lift her spirits. To put her at ease. To make her feel good about herself again. To help her rise above the low blow her ex-husband had struck and make her completely forget Rob and his pregnant new wife were anywhere around.

And all the while he'd kept both her and himself well stocked with margaritas.

Yes, he'd had a whole lot to drink, too. Which had no doubt contributed to the fact that they'd ended up together...for the entire night.

"Northbridge. Fifteen miles," Clair read aloud.

Take a deep breath and blow it out. Take a deep breath and blow it out....

It would have been so much easier if she hadn't let Cassie talk her into staying at that reunion, Clair thought now. Or if, once she'd stayed, she'd continued not knowing Ben Walker existed—the way she'd hardly known he existed ten years ago.

But oh, brother had she known Ben Walker existed. With those smoky blue-green eyes and that deliciously wicked quirk that curled the corner of this mouth when he was showing that hint of devil that still lurked beneath the surface.

Clair had most certainly known he existed that night in June.

Not that she had a vivid memory of too much more than that when it came to Ben Walker, though. Beyond the way he looked and being with him during the early portion of the evening, she hardly remembered anything. She definitely didn't recall how they'd gotten to her room at the local bed-and-breakfast where she was registered. And from that point, the rest of the night was just a blur she couldn't bring into any kind of clear focus no matter how hard she tried.

But the next morning? Now *that* she remembered.

She'd been mortified to wake up in bed with a man she barely knew.

So mortified that while he was still sleeping, she'd run out on him without a word, without leaving him a note, without a remnant of herself left behind—as if that might erase what had happened between them. She'd left him in her room, thrown her suitcase in the back seat of her car and driven straight home, hoping she would never have to see Ben Walker again.

Hoping she could just forget that reunion, that trip to Northbridge, that one night. Hoping she could just forget it all.

And wouldn't *that* have been nice….

But instead, a month after the reunion the Realtor who had been trying to sell the Northbridge School for Boys on her behalf had called to say he had a buyer. A buyer named Ben Walker.

Okaaay, she'd said, hoping the transaction could be done by proxy, that she still wouldn't have to face him.

There was just one glitch.

Since her father was no longer living and able to turn the place over to the new owner himself, Clair had told the Realtor she was willing to do it. Only she'd told the Realtor that *before* there was even a buyer and before she'd had any idea that that new owner would be Ben Walker. And he was taking her up on the offer.

The offer to personally return to Northbridge to orient him on the workings of the place and the social service requirements he would have to meet for a placement facility of that nature.

So there she was, the week before Labor Day, once again on her way to Northbridge. Embarrassed that she'd had a few too many drinks and spent the night not only with a virtual stranger, but a virtual stranger who was her friend's brother. Embarrassed that she'd ditched that brother the next morning. And carrying with her the consequences of her actions.

"Welcome to Northbridge, Montana," she said sarcastically, once again reading a sign as she turned right, off the nearly deserted rural highway.

It was two more miles down a road that ran between matching fields of cornstalks that formed tall walls on either side and cast long shadows in the late evening light. Then the fields gave way to ancient oak trees lush with green leaves before she actually reached the town itself. And Main Street.

Clair pulled into the first place she came to on Main Street—the service station, which, along with the bus station across the street, was the beginning of that end of the town proper.

She didn't need gas. She just needed to stop. So she parked alongside the station rather than at the pumps and got out.

The front door to the station was open, even though it was long after the scheduled 6:00 p.m. closing time, and so was the big garage door where a truck with its hood raised was apparently being worked on in the mechanic's bay. But no one was anywhere to be seen. Clair headed for the restroom, which she knew would only be locked if someone else was using it.

No one was, so she stepped inside and turned on the light before she leaned back against the door, closed her eyes and once again advised herself to breathe.

This wasn't the way things were supposed to work out, she couldn't help thinking as it began to sink in that she really was in Northbridge again.

Her dad was supposed to live to a ripe old age and go on running the school until he was ready to turn it over to someone else himself.

She was supposed to be married. She was supposed to have a big family to bring back and raise in Northbridge so her father could be included, so her father could revel in his role as grandfather. She was supposed to finish her own life here in Northbridge. And she was supposed to do it all with Rob.

But that wasn't the way things had worked out.

And if there was one thing she'd learned in the last year of having her whole life turned topsy-turvy, it was that she had to deal with whatever came of the latest topsy-turvy turn.

"So deal," she told herself. But that was easier said than done.

Still, she was determined to manage to the best of her ability.

So she took one more deep breath, blew it out and opened her eyes.

If there was a cleaner gas station bathroom in the country, Clair had never been in it and just the sight of that spotless space made her smile.

Northbridge.

Where else would the station owner's mother come in to personally scrub the restroom and keep a crocheted doily across the top of the toilet tank?

Clair pushed off the door and after using the pristine facilities, she grabbed the heart-shaped, strawberry-scented soap from a ceramic dish on the edge of the sink to wash her hands. Then she dried them with paper towel taken from a roll held on the wall by a dispenser with two brown bears perched atop either end of the bar.

And all the while she kept thinking, *only in Northbridge....*

She tossed the used paper towel into a wicker basket, and glanced at herself in the mirror above the sink.

It had been a long drive from Denver, through Wyoming to Montana, and she'd been traveling since dawn. It was now after eight o'clock, and she decided she looked like someone who had been behind the wheel of a car all that time.

Some repair work was in order, she decided.

She grabbed a tissue and blotted her face, paying particular attention to her forehead since she'd just had her very wavy, honey-blond hair cut short—including the bangs that were now barely below her hairline and left most of her brow showing.

With that done, she opened her purse and removed a small makeup bag. After applying a light dusting of blush onto the crests of her high cheekbones and into the hollows below them, she passed the brush lightly along the underside of her jawline.

She was grateful to have the skin and the bone structure she had—neither would put her on the cover of a magazine but at least her complexion had always been clear and between her cheekbones and jawline there was some definition.

She wished her eyelashes were longer though, and reapplied mascara to help give the illusion that they were. And as she did, she was glad to see that the whites around her almost-purple irises weren't bloodshot as they had been the week before when the latest topsy-turvy turn her life had taken had kept her from sleeping for several nights.

A light coating of lip gloss didn't alter the natural pink of lips that she also wished were a bit fuller. And for about the hundredth time since she'd had her hair cut, she wondered if it had been wise to go so drastically from shoulder-length to a curly cap that the stylist had proclaimed sporty and cute and so much more au courant than the way she'd been wearing it.

Actually, what she was wondering was what Ben Walker would think of her haircut. But she curbed that thought the minute she realized she was having it. Rob hated short hair and would have had a fit—which had probably influenced her decision to do it. But once she *had* gone ahead with the new style, it had seemed liberating to do something for herself. She certainly wasn't going to start fretting over the approval or disapproval of another man.

"Sporty and cute and au courant," she said, finding that repeating the hairstylist's words and taking stock of her new look somehow helped bolster her. It also helped remind her that she was her own woman now. Strong enough to have withstood a lot in the past year. Resilient. Capable. Competent. She could take care of herself and whatever else she needed to take care of. So what if things hadn't turned out the way they were supposed to? She could handle it. She could handle anything.

At least she hoped she could when her stomach did the little lurch it had been doing for the past few weeks, and she remembered that the latest topsy-turvy turn was a big one.

But still, now that she had actually arrived in Northbridge, and had freshened up and reassured herself that she would be okay, she felt better than she had driving into town.

Even if she was back in Northbridge to hand over her father's school.

Even if she was divorced.

Even if she'd made one of the biggest miscalculations of her entire life when she'd spent the night with Ben Walker in June and became pregnant with his baby…!

* * *

The Northbridge School for Boys was just outside of town to the west. When Clair turned off the road onto the drive that led up to it, she stopped the car so she could have a moment to look at the place her father had loved.

The original house was a flat-faced, three-story wooden box painted pale yellow and trimmed in white. The building stood about a quarter of a mile from the road in a circle of elm trees that seemed to protect it.

The house and trees blocked the view of the barn, chicken coop, pigsties and paddocks behind the main building that made the school a working ranch. The small caretaker's cottage where she and her father had made their own home was also to the rear of the main house and out of sight from the front approach.

Clair stopped between two matching white rail fences that bordered the drive on both sides. Within the confines of those fenced pastures there were horses to her right and dairy cows to her left. The fence gave way to a circular drive, and a lush green lawn carpeted the ground to the flower beds that decorated the space immediately in front of the house.

Those who didn't know what the place was or didn't get close enough to read the small brass plaque that announced it was the Northbridge School for Boys would never guess it wasn't merely the pastoral estate of a gentleman farmer.

But that had suited her father. He'd always said that even though it might be an institutional facility, he wanted it to be homey and welcoming and something the boys would learn to take pride in. And because that wasn't always a simple task with troubled kids, his tool-box had been at the ready to make repairs—always assisted by whoever had wreaked the damage.

This was the first time Clair had been to the school since her father's untimely death from a sudden heart attack. She hadn't been able to face staying there alone when she'd come to the reunion, but she'd planned to at least drive out and have a look at things.

Instead she'd made her abrupt departure from the bed-and-breakfast, from Northbridge—and from Ben Walker—without ever doing that.

But now that she was there she was pleased to see that the place the Realtor had said was beginning to show some signs of neglect over the past year, looked as well tended as it had when her father had been at the helm.

No doubt that was thanks to Ben Walker. The Realtor had told Clair that as soon as the sale had closed he'd begun to work on the place so he could open this month.

He'd also moved in—again, according to the Realtor who had told her that Ben Walker would be living on-site just as she and her father had. But the Realtor had also said that Ben Walker would give up the cottage to Clair while she was there, to spare her the expense of the bed-and-breakfast. During that time, he would stay in the main building.

So there she was.

Inside, Ben Walker was waiting for her.

She couldn't imagine what he must think of her. She was just reasonably sure it couldn't be anything good. But there was nothing she could do about that now so she decided she might as well get this show on the road.

Take a deep breath and blow it out.

Clair took her own silent advice again.

Then she drove the rest of the way to the building.

Apparently Ben Walker wasn't watching for her because the big mahogany door remained closed as she parked, turned off the engine and got out of the car with her suitcase.

When she reached the front door she automatically put her hand on the knob to open it before it occurred to her that the place didn't belong to her—or to her father—any longer and that she couldn't just go in.

So she pulled her hand away and rang the bell instead, feeling a whole new layer of awkwardness.

But when the door opened it wasn't Ben Walker on the other side of it. It was Cassie Walker.

"Hey there, stranger!" Clair's old friend greeted her with a smile and a big hug. "I was hoping you'd get here before I left, and you just barely made it."

"Cassie!" Clair responded with a full measure of relief echoing in her voice. She hadn't expected her friend to be there but the fact that Cassie was helped immensely.

"Come in, come in," Cassie encouraged. But despite the invitation, she didn't make way for Clair because, as if the change in Clair had just registered, she said, "You cut your hair."

"I did," Clair confirmed, self-consciously fingering the short curls at her nape.

"It's so cute. I love it on you. Even though I'm still mad at you."

"You're mad at me?"

"For the reunion. I can't believe you left that night without telling me you were going and then didn't even call before going back to Denver the next day. I don't care if you *were* in a hurry to escape before you had to see Rob again."

A second wave of relief washed through Clair. She'd called her friend a few days after the reunion, worrying that Cassie's twin might have told her that he'd spent the night with Clair. But when it had become clear that Ben hadn't said anything about it, Clair had given her friend the likeliest excuse—not wanting to see Rob again—to explain her hasty departure both from the reunion and from Northbridge the following morning. But for just a moment, Clair thought maybe Ben had told Cassie belatedly and her friend was genuinely angry. It was good that that didn't seem to be the truth.

"Maybe we'll have time to visit and catch up while I'm here now," Clair said to appease her friend.

"I'm counting on it," Cassie said. Then she obviously recalled that they were still standing in the doorway and said, "Oh, look at me—I told you to come in and then went right on blocking the door." But this time she stepped out of the way.

Clair took her suitcase with her into the foyer and

while Cassie closed the door behind her, Clair glanced around.

From what she could see, Ben Walker had left the lower level of the house just as her father had—just as it had been when the building had served as a private home. The large foyer had a hardwood floor and paneled walls with archways cut out of them to connect a living room to the right and a recreation room that housed a reproduction of an antique pool table to the left.

There was also a broad staircase directly across from the door, with hallways leading to the rear of the house on both sides of it. The space above the foyer was open to the second level where the staircase branched off in both directions to rise to the third floor.

Cassie aimed her chin up the stairs then and shouted, "Ben! Are you coming down? Clair's here."

He must have already been on his way before that because no sooner were the words out than his voice came in answer from the left branch of the staircase.

"On my way," he said as work-booted feet and long, jean-clad legs with impressively muscular thighs came into view, followed by a leather tool belt slung low on a pair of narrow hips, a V-shaped torso with muscular chest, mile-wide shoulders and bulging biceps that were all barely contained in a plain white T-shirt.

"It was you who said you heard a car on the drive and then what do you do but disappear," Cassie said to him as he reached the second-floor landing.

But not even that brought his gaze to them. Instead,

stalled on the upper landing, he was so intent on replacing tools in the loops of his tool belt it was as if Cassie and Clair were only incidental.

"I wanted to close that paint can before I forgot," he muttered.

Both Cassie and Clair stood there watching him, and as she did it struck Clair that he was even better-looking than she remembered—something she hadn't thought was possible.

And it wasn't only the bounty of his body that was remarkable. His dark, sable-brown hair was short all over and in a sexy disarray that made it impossible to tell if it was by design or nature. His features were the kind that a camera would love—stark and chiseled, with a square brow, a sharp jaw that cradled a chin with the slightest cleft in the center and a nose that was thin and perfectly aquiline.

His skin was smooth and sun-bronzed, his lean cheeks were shadowed with a day's growth of beard that made him look appealingly scruffy, and when he finally finished hooking his tools through their allotted loops and cast his attention in the direction of the foyer, the blue-green of his eyes was so intense Clair thought she could feel his gaze settling on her.

But not so much as the hint of emotion was evident in his deep voice when he said, "Hello, Clair."

Then he finally came the rest of the way down the steps on legs that bowed a little and carried him on a slow swagger that had just a hint of insolence to it.

And all of a sudden Clair found her throat so dry she had trouble saying, "Hi."

His eyes remained on her but he didn't say anything else, and Clair wasn't sure if she was imagining it or if there was a sort of challenge in his expression. In his whole stance.

But if there was she didn't know what he was challenging her to or how to meet it, and she was grateful when Cassie filled the gap.

"Have you eaten? Are you hungry? Thirsty? We had Chinese food and there are leftovers. And I made a pitcher of lemonade a little while ago."

"Just the lemonade sounds good," Clair managed.

Cassie checked her wristwatch. "I only have a few minutes before I need to leave for a committee meeting. I'm helping Ben with things around here because he's down to the wire, but I also have stuff going on for fall semester at the college—although admittedly as a student advisor I won't be swamped there until the kids show up so I'll be in and out with you guys the whole time you're here. Anyway, how about if I pour while Ben takes your suitcase out to the cottage?"

The only part of what Cassie said that registered with Clair was the part about Cassie only staying a few more minutes. And that fact made her suffer a fresh bout of panic. But she didn't let it show. Instead she said a weak, "Okay."

Cassie linked her arm through Clair's then and headed for the kitchen, chattering about Northbridge going international with the opening of Ling's Chinese Palace restaurant.

It wasn't like Cassie to be so frenzied, and Clair wondered if her friend was responding to the tension in the air. But she was too on-edge herself to do more than let Cassie carry her along.

And all the while she was watching Ben as he walked ahead of them with her suitcase, knowing she shouldn't be looking at his great rear end, and that she certainly shouldn't be trying futilely to remember what it had looked like naked.

But it was only when they reached the large kitchen at the back of the house and Ben went out the sliding door that she managed to stop thinking about his derriere and focus on something else. On the kitchen itself.

The kitchen was as it had always been—a big, wide-open space with commercial-size appliances, and very little in the way of decor—with the exception of the backsplash tiles with the floral motif. There was a marble island counter with barstools on one side of it, and, for dining purposes, there was a long rectangular table with picnic-bench-style seating.

Cassie motioned Clair to one of the barstools, and then went to the refrigerator.

"It's hard for you to be here again with your dad gone, isn't it?" Cassie said when her brother was out of sight and earshot, letting Clair know that that was what her friend attributed the tension to.

"A little," Clair admitted because that was also a factor in her stress.

"Will you be okay alone in the cottage? I really wish you could stay at my place, but with my roommate's brother sleeping on our couch right now I know you wouldn't be comfortable. My offer is still good, though, to come out here and stay with you, if you want."

It was a tempting offer—not only because then Cassie would provide a constant diversion from Ben, but because Clair would have liked to spend time with her friend.

But she had a purpose other than helping Ben Walker get the school started and that purpose would only be served *without* a diversion.

So Clair said, "I'll be okay. You don't have to baby-sit me."

"It wouldn't be *baby-sitting,*" Cassie assured. "And I don't mind if you need me."

"Thanks, but, no. Really. I'm fine."

Cassie accepted that, brought Clair the glass of lemonade and then pointed to the wall clock. "I hate to rush off the minute you get here but I have to."

"It's okay," Clair lied.

"I'll be back tomorrow, and Ben will take good care of you in the meantime—won't you?"

Clair hadn't heard him come back and since she was facing away from the sliding door she had to look over her shoulder to make sure that's who Cassie was talking to.

"Uh-huh," he answered.

But apparently it was answer enough for Cassie because it prompted her to say, "All right then, I better go. I'll see you both tomorrow."

Clair and Ben responded with goodbyes of their own and then all of a sudden they were alone. In a silence Clair thought was heavy enough to be tangible.

But she didn't know what to say. She didn't know whether to launch into an explanation of what had gone through her mind at the reunion and the next morning. Or to make excuses for herself. Or to try to convince him that her actions that night were unusual in the extreme— which they were.

Or maybe she should just act as if nothing had happened at all….

"Long drive from Denver," he said then, interrupting the silence and her racing thoughts as he went to stand on the opposite side of the island. He stretched his arms wide and grabbed hold of the edges of the countertop.

"It is a long drive," Clair agreed. "But I got a really early start this morning and it was a nice day for traveling. Sunny but not too hot."

She couldn't believe she was actually talking about the weather. Still, she just couldn't bring herself to delve into anything deeper.

And then he did.

He said, "She doesn't know—Cassie, that is—about what happened at the reunion. Between you and me. Nobody does." He paused, made a sound that wasn't quite a laugh, and added, "Including me in a lot of respects."

"I'm not all that clear myself. Even about the parts I remember," Clair admitted, staring at the beads of water on the outside of her lemonade glass because she couldn't look him in the eye.

"We did have a lot to drink that night," he allowed, making it easier for her. At least up to a point. "But the next morning...I was sobered up by then, you must have been, too."

"In more ways than one," she said half under her breath.

"What does that mean?" he asked anyway.

Whether she wanted to explain or not, apparently she was going to have to so Clair didn't see any reason to fight it and merely gave in.

"That's just not something I do—or have *ever done*—spending the night with someone like that," she said haltingly because what she'd done was so foreign to her that she didn't even know how to refer to her behavior. "I..." She had to clear her throat. "Before that I'd only...*been*...with Rob."

"Rob?"

"Cabot. Rob Cabot? My husband—*ex*-husband?"

Ben shook his head and shrugged. "Am I supposed to know him?"

"We all went to high school together. He was there, at the reunion. With his new wife. He wasn't supposed to be. He said he wasn't going. It was the first time I'd seen him since our divorce, and the whole thing is still so strange to me and it just hit home and… Well, that's why Cassie asked you to keep me company," Clair said, looking for any kind of light to dawn in him.

But it never did. "All I know is that I was having a lousy time that night and never should have let my sister talk me into going. I was like a fish out of water that last semester of school and I was just as much a fish out of water that night. But when I told her I was leaving she said you were having a rotten time, too, and asked if I would sit with you until she could get back to you."

Which Cassie hadn't been able to do.

"So you didn't know—" Clair cut herself off, not wanting to get into the subject of Rob and that night in the middle of the rest of this. "And it wasn't just a pity—"

She couldn't believe that train of thought had found voice. *Her voice.*

But it made him smile. A slow, lopsided, private-joke-kind of smile that somehow managed to instantly dissipate a lot of the tension in the room.

"You thought that whole night was a…out of pity?"

"I thought it was possible," she confessed quietly.

Now he was trying to keep from grinning and in the struggle his eyebrows arched up over the bridge of his nose in a way that made him look innocent and devilish all at once. "I didn't know anything was going on that I should pity you for," he said.

"Good."

"But I have to admit you have me curious now."

"Too bad," she said, her tone making it clear she had no intention of satisfying that curiosity.

For some reason that made him laugh. Which, in turn, helped even more of the tension evaporate.

"Okay," he said, his stance relaxing, too, as he let his weight shift to one hip and stood up straighter to cross his arms over his chest. "So is that why you disappeared the next morning? Because you thought I'd only been there out of pity?"

"No, I was just… Well, I was crazy that next morning. I couldn't believe I'd actually done what I'd done. I just…ran."

He didn't respond immediately. In fact he didn't respond for so long that Clair hazarded a glance up at him.

He was watching her. Studying her. As if he were trying to decide whether or not to accept what she was telling him.

Finally he said, "I didn't appreciate it."

Nothing like being blunt.

But Clair knew she had it coming.

"I'm sorry. I know it was probably bad etiquette or something. I just didn't know what to do or say or how to act or…anything. All I could think to do was to go home."

That sounded lame. But it was the truth.

He either realized that or opted for letting her off the hook, though, because after another moment of studying her he said, "How about we forget the reunion ever happened and start over?"

She couldn't *completely* forget it. But, for the time

being, Clair thought it might be best to put it on a back burner.

"I'd like to start over," she said, agreeing to at least that part of his suggestion.

"Then let's do that."

Those aqua eyes were warmer than they'd been since her arrival and that warmth made her feel much, much better.

"I can tell you're worn-out from the drive, and since I want to get an early start tomorrow I told Cassie I'd fix the two of you breakfast at seven-thirty, if that's all right with you?"

"Sure, seven-thirty is fine."

"Okay, then, since you've had a long trip and we're starting early tomorrow, how about if I walk you out to the cottage, let you unpack and get some rest? And we'll consider tomorrow day one?"

"I'd like that."

"Okay, it's a deal."

He held out his hand for her to shake and she took it without thinking that the feel of it might cause anything to erupt in her.

But it did. That perfectly innocent handshake that any two strangers might have shared made her extremely aware of the heat of his skin, the strength of his grip, the sensuality of his touch—things she didn't want to be aware of at all.

And just the fact that she was, spurred her to say, "I

don't even think you should walk me to the cottage. I'll just slip out as if I was never here, and we'll be that much closer to putting the reunion behind us and starting over."

"You're sure?" he asked as she got down from the barstool in a hurry.

"Positive. You don't know me. I'm not here," she said on the way to the sliding door.

He followed her that far anyway, reaching around in front of her to open the door, keeping his hand high up on the edge of it and leaning against it as she went outside.

"Okay. See you around, stranger," he said from behind her.

"Maybe. If you're lucky," she countered, stealing one more glance over her shoulder at him and finding him smiling that private-joke smile again.

It made her want to stay.

How did that happen? she asked herself as she gave him a little wave and turned away to head down the short brick path to the cottage.

But she didn't have an answer. She only knew that somehow she'd gone from nearly hyperventilating at just the thought of seeing Ben Walker again, to actually being tempted to linger a while longer with him. And that the effect he had on her was like no other any man had ever had on her before.

Although maybe his having unusual effects on her

shouldn't have come as such a surprise under the circumstances.

Circumstances in which he'd managed to conquer her infertility.

Chapter Two

Ben hadn't gone for a run in a while. He'd been too busy getting the school ready to open. But the following morning he was up earlier than usual anyway, and he decided it might do him some good.

So he pulled on a pair of cutoff jeans and his ratty old gray sleeves-torn-out T-shirt and, after some stretches to warm up, he set off just as the sun was making its first appearance.

He'd started running for exercise as a teenager. Exercise itself was something the ACA—the Arizona Center for Adolescents—had required. One of the many things required there. But running had given him the only sense of freedom he'd had in placement—even though he'd had to do it with a staff member along. So it had been something he'd adopted early on, something he'd stuck with ever since.

It just felt good. It helped him ease stress. It helped clear his head.

And right now he *needed* his head cleared. It was full of lists of things he had to get done so the school could open in the next two weeks. Full of guidelines, codes and requirements he had to meet. Full of questions he had for Clair Cabot.

Full of Clair Cabot...

Okay sure, she was really what had him up and running this morning. Thoughts of her. He might as well admit it. Why not, when thoughts of her weren't such a strange occurrence since the reunion anyway? Since he'd woken the next morning to discover she'd left him behind like a dirty shirt. In fact she'd been on his mind so much that trying *not* to think about her almost seemed like his new hobby.

But now that he had a glimmer of an idea of what might be going on with her, he really wanted her cleared out of his mind.

Damn Cassie for setting him up like that, he thought as he increased his speed a little.

His sister hadn't told him that Clair was divorced—let alone *newly* divorced.

And she should have. Cassie, of all people, knew how he felt about playing rebound guy for anyone. She knew he'd learned the hard way not to get within a hundred yards of any woman not long—*long*—past a breakup. Which was probably why she hadn't told him that the reason that her friend was having a lousy time at the reunion had something to do with an ex-husband and his new wife. Cassie had to have known that if he'd had that fact at his disposal there would have been no chance in hell that he would have helped Cassie out by trying to cheer up Clair Cabot that night.

Let alone gone back to her room with her.

Or slept with her.

And opened himself up for something like what had happened when she'd hightailed it out of that room in the cold light of day. Hightailed it completely out of town without so much as a note or a phone number written in lipstick on the mirror or an *it's been nice knowing you....*

Yes, it was good to finally find out that he hadn't done something wrong that night. Not that he'd been able to figure out how that might have been the case when it had actually seemed like they'd both had a pretty fantastic night together.

But he *had* had a lot to drink beforehand and when Clair had disappeared on him like that it had left him wondering if he'd been mistaken, if things between them hadn't been as amazing as he'd thought.

That was the point in situations like these though, he reminded himself. The point was that no matter how fantastic, how amazing things were, when one person was fresh out of another relationship, it just didn't matter. A rebound was a rebound was a rebound.

And now even just assuming that that was the case with Clair, he wished he'd left that reunion before he'd ever set eyes on her.

Or at least before Cassie had teamed him up with her—he'd actually noticed Clair well in advance of his sister's request to keep her friend occupied.

He'd noticed Clair in the school parking lot when she'd first arrived at the reunion. Cassie had forgotten the yearbook and sent him to her car to get it. As he was leaning inside the open passenger door trying to find it, Clair had pulled into the spot in front of Cassie's, nose-to-nose, which had started a series of glances at her from Ben—one, two, three glances....

He hadn't recognized her or had any idea that she was the friend his sister was excited to see. During those last few months he'd been home before graduation he'd probably only crossed paths with her a few times. And that had been ten years ago. Besides, he'd been so busy trying to toe the line then that he hadn't had time to be involved with his sister's active social life.

But that evening at the reunion had been different.

He wasn't sure why. Maybe she hadn't looked the same ten years ago. Or maybe she had and it just hadn't struck him then. But in that initial glance at her in June he'd liked the look of her. Which was a little odd in it-self when he ordinarily went for dark-haired women.

But the sun had hit her just right when she'd pulled into that parking spot, shining through her side window and glimmering in the golden-blond streaks of her hair.

And all of a sudden glistening blond hair had looked uncommonly good to him.

So uncommonly good to him that he wasn't sure he liked that she'd cut most of it off now.

He remembered her flawless skin—he guessed the shorter hair *did* show off more of that, anyway. Flawless skin with healthy pink tones dusting high cheekbones that somehow gave her an air of exotic innocence—if there was such a thing—then and now.

But it hadn't only been her shiny blond hair, fine bone structure and porcelain skin that had spurred him to take a second glance at her that night in June.

He'd stolen the second glance when she'd opened her car door and long, shapely legs had made their appearance below it. Then she'd closed the driver's door, and he'd been treated to the view of long, shapely legs easing into a cute little body with just enough up front and behind.

She'd opened the rear door to get something from the back seat and he'd averted his gaze again. He'd gone on with his search under Cassie's seat for the yearbook.

But once he'd found the yearbook he'd backed out of the car just as Clair Cabot had closed her rear door, too. And something about that simultaneous movement had been enough of an excuse to draw yet a third glance at her.

She'd looked directly at him that time, meeting his eyes with hers. And holy cow, what eyes they were!

They were the color of the lilacs that grew on the

bush alongside his mother's house. *Purple* eyes. Clair Cabot had big, deep, dark purple eyes that still managed to be bright and sparkling in spite of all that depth of color. Eyes that had held him transfixed for a moment and almost unable to break that hold. Or certainly *unwilling* to…

And then, with the softest-looking, rose petal lips, she'd smiled at him. Tentatively. Uncertainly. Obviously wondering if he was someone she should remember. But with enough warmth to make him glad he'd gone to the reunion after all.

He'd actually been thinking about introducing himself to her, wondering if he would discover that she was someone he'd known all along. But before he'd had the chance, two other women had spotted her and rushed to say hello, calling her by name.

That was how he'd found out who she was.

Clair Cabot.

Ah, Cassie's friend…

She'd turned away from him to talk to the other women then, and Ben couldn't very well hang around waiting for another opportunity to speak to her, so he'd returned to the school gym without saying anything.

Only once he was there, he'd kept an eye on the door, watching for her, still considering approaching her when she came inside. Wondering if he should pretend he remembered her as his sister's friend….

Except that when she had come inside, she'd gone straight to the reception table to get her name tag and it had seemed as if she'd had an awkward exchange with another couple there. Old enemies—that's the impression he'd had. Probably a high school rivalry or something. Then she'd disappeared in a hurry into the girls' locker room.

And that was the last he'd seen of her for more than an hour.

It just hadn't been the last he'd thought of her.

Which was probably why, when, by pure coincidence, Cassie had asked him to keep her friend Clair company some time later, he'd agreed. Without asking why. Without asking anything. Just feeling a little thrill that he was going to get to see Clair Cabot again and talk to her after all.

Ben pushed his speed up to an almost punishing rate for the last leg of his run, thinking that regardless of the fact that he'd been glad his sister had asked that particular favor of him at the time, Cassie still should have known better. She should have at least warned him that her friend was suffering some kind of post-divorce fallout so he would have had his guard up. So it wouldn't have mattered how great Clair looked or how funny or sweet she'd been, or how much he'd ultimately enjoyed her company.

So he wouldn't have done something as dumb as spend the night with her.

The school came into view just then, and the sight of it made him think *and that's another thing...*

The school. The Northbridge School for Boys was

his priority. His number-one priority. He'd reminded himself of that every time Clair Cabot and her running out on him had come to mind over the past two months.

The school was something he'd wanted to do since the day he'd been released from placement himself. It had been his dream, his goal, to work with kids who were like he'd been, and to do it the way he felt—the way he *knew*—it should be done.

Now that he'd reached that goal, he was devoting himself to it and to the boys he accepted into the program. It wasn't something he would do halfheartedly, that was for sure. And until the school was well established, until everything was in order and it was almost running itself, he couldn't let himself be distracted. Not by anything…or anyone.

And Clair Cabot—purple eyes and blond hair and cute little body or not—had to be strictly relegated to business status, he told himself firmly.

She was there to show him how her father ran the place. To walk him through the billing procedures and teach him how to do the necessary paperwork. She was there to fill him in on what had to be done for social services to certify him.

But that was all she was there for—business.

In fact, tending to business was the reason he'd made the suggestion that they start over—so they could put the night they'd spent together behind them and focus on what needed to be done now.

And when that business was taken care of, she could

go back where she'd come from—where she'd run to the morning after the reunion—and he could forget about her.

Except, of course, he hadn't been able to forget her.

That thought brought him full circle in his musings just as his run came to an end.

So, he asked himself as he walked the final few yards up the drive to cool down, if he hadn't been successful at forgetting Clair Cabot before, how was he going to do it when she left again?

He wasn't really sure.

He hoped that maybe it would help that he would be occupied with the opening of the school. That maybe he would just be too busy to think about her.

Or maybe, knowing now that not only was she someone who might disappear on him the way she had at the reunion but also that she was in the inordinately risky newly divorced category, would help cool his jets.

But deep down he didn't feel too confident in any of those possibilities.

Because he wasn't sure those jets she'd fired up two months ago would ever cool down.

Especially when so many of his thoughts about her came complete with memories of what had been one of the most incredible nights of his life....

It had taken Clair a while to fall asleep Monday night. Between being in the small, two-bedroom cottage where she'd lived with her dad, and all the mixed emotions she had about seeing Ben again, she'd been awake until after 1:00 a.m.

As a result she was late getting up Tuesday morning. And even though she only took a quick shower and raced through dressing in jeans and a crop-sleeved crew-neck T-shirt, she still arrived in the kitchen of the main house after both Ben and Cassie.

"I'm so sorry to keep you guys waiting," Clair apologized. "I overslept."

"You didn't keep me waiting," Cassie assured from where she was standing at the entrance to the kitchen. "I just got here myself."

"Okay then, I'm sorry to keep *you* waiting," Clair amended, aiming that portion of the apology at Ben, who was sitting at one end of the long, rectangular table.

"Don't let it happen again or I'll have to give you extra chores and three days restriction," he joked, clearly referring to a punishment he intended to mete out to any of his rule-breaking charges.

Then he raised his coffee cup and pointed it in the direction of the coffeemaker on the counter. "Help yourselves, ladies. This is fresh-brewed and there's scrambled eggs, bacon and toast staying warm in the oven."

"What kind of host are you?" Cassie chastised as she came farther into the room, sounding very sisterly. "You're supposed to get up and serve your guests."

This time Ben used his mug to motion toward the two unused place settings on either side of him. "I would have served you both if you'd have shown up when we agreed. But I've already had my breakfast and finished my second cup of coffee. Now I'm going down to the basement to get started while you two eat."

"Are we *that* late?" Cassie asked Clair.

"About an hour," Clair confirmed. "He told me seven-thirty and it's eight-twenty-five."

"I suppose we can't fault you, then," Cassie conceded as Ben stood, then took his breakfast dishes to rinse and put in the dishwasher.

Clair marveled at the fact that he didn't seem angry with them.

"See you both downstairs," he said then, disappearing through the door that concealed the steps leading to the basement.

"Looks like we're on our own," Cassie said.

"I think that's what we get," Clair confided as she removed the platter of food from the oven, taking it to the table as Cassie brought the coffeepot.

Clair bypassed the coffee to avoid the caffeine, and she and Cassie shared the remaining breakfast foods.

As they did, they only discussed what they'd decided to do today—retrieving, inventorying and putting away the bed linens, towels and other necessary items that had been packed in boxes and stored in the basement when the school had been closed after Clair's father's death. Then they joined Ben for what proceeded to be a very busy day of climbing up and down steps, sorting, counting, discarding anything that was too worn, and assigning closets, shelves and drawers to everything they kept.

Clair didn't hesitate to let Ben know how her dad had organized things when he was in charge, but ultimately it was Ben's decision as to what he wanted where, and she didn't argue with him when he changed a few things.

They worked until well after dark that evening, and when they were finished, they were exhausted. It was too late to prepare anything substantial for dinner by then, so they had pizza and salads delivered.

They ate in the living room around the coffee table before Cassie confessed she was beat and left Clair and Ben still sitting on the floor—Clair with her back resting against the front of a leather easy chair and Ben angled so that one long arm was braced atop the matching sofa cushion so he was partially facing her.

Ben hadn't had much to say most of the day—at least not in the way of anything that didn't pertain to the work they were doing. It had been Cassie and Clair who had chatted while he had basically hung back, more involved with the heavy lifting and the matters at hand than in socializing.

That fact left Clair uncertain if he might prefer that she say good-night, too, now that his sister was gone. But Ben surprised and pleased her a little by not giving her the chance to make her own exit yet. Instead, he pointed his chin toward an old, battered cardboard box they'd brought up from the basement earlier in the day when they'd discovered it contained some of Clair's childhood memorabilia.

"Did you find any treasures in there?" he asked.

"Like a long-lost antique I could take to one of those road shows they do on television and find out it's worth thousands of dollars?"

"Maybe."

"Unfortunately, no. There are just some dolls and doll clothes, a stuffed dog with one ear chewed off, and my first patent-leather Easter shoes. Nothing of any great value, only some mementos that somehow got stuck downstairs, I guess."

"Who chewed the ear off the dog?" he asked with the hint of a smile shining out from the scruffy-looking day's growth of beard that was reminiscent of what he'd had when he'd greeted her the evening before because he'd been too busy to shave a second time today, too.

"I've been told that I dragged the dog everywhere and gnawed on his ear whenever I was feeling shy or upset," she informed him.

"Can I see?" he asked with what Clair thought was a hint of mischief in his expression.

"It isn't pretty," she warned, giving tacit approval.

Ben pulled the box closer and peered inside, surveying the contents.

Clair watched him.

He was dressed much as he had been the day before in jeans and a T-shirt—this one gray. But the T-shirt fitted him like a second skin, accentuating the well-developed muscles of his torso, and she couldn't help wondering how anyone could look quite that good with so little effort.

And he definitely looked good.

After a moment of peering at the contents of the box, he reached in and extracted the dog as if he'd made his decision about what piece of Halloween candy to pick from the bowl.

The dog was ragged and soiled and, indeed, missing one ear.

"You must have been really shy or really upset," he observed with a wry half smile.

"Potty-training can be hard on a person," Clair joked defensively.

"How long did you drag this poor fella around?"

"Until I was seventeen." She'd delivered that joke deadpan but he realized she really was kidding and laughed.

"You weren't potty-trained until you were seventeen?"

"Sixteen and a half but I still kept Charmagne around until I was seventeen."

Ben chuckled again. "Charmagne?"

"That's her name. She's Charmagne the Shih-tzu."

"And she's a girl, huh?" he said, turning her over with a devilry that no doubt helped earn him his bad-boy reputation.

But Clair laughed anyway. "Charmagne is a girl's name, so yes, she's a girl. You'll just have to take my word for it."

"No, I can see that you're right," he said as if he'd been able to tell.

He set the stuffed toy on the coffee table as if he

wanted to keep it in sight, and then settled his gaze on her again. "So this stuff is from before you came here."

"Long before."

"I kept wondering today what it was like for you when you grew up here."

"It was okay."

"Not a rave review. Are you warning me that if I ever have kids of my own I should raise them somewhere else?"

Clair shied away from the if-he-ever-had-kids-of-his-own part of his question as if it were a live electrical wire loose from its moorings. But she did answer his question about her own time at the school.

"I didn't hate it here. I guess what I sort of resented—and really, only *sort of*—was that no matter what happened, at any hour of the day or night, my dad insisted that he be hands-on involved in it."

"For instance…"

"For instance, my sixteenth birthday. He promised me a dinner out, just the two of us, at the best restaurant in Billings. Only just when our salads were served he got a call from the school—he always left orders when he was going to leave the grounds that he was to be called for everything and anything that happened, and even if he didn't hear from whoever was in charge when he was gone, he called to check with them every hour. Anyway, that night, one of the kids had had a nightmare, but even though it was already under control, we had to cancel the rest of our dinner and come back."

Ben made a face. "It's great for the kids in the program that he cared so much. But definitely lousy for you."

"It wouldn't have been so bad if it had only been real crises that he'd dropped everything to attend to. But it seemed like once we came here, he put every little thing ahead of me. Or at least that's how it felt. Maybe he was throwing himself into his work to deal with his grief over my mom's death, but—"

"I knew your dad was a widower but I never knew how your mom died."

"A city bus ran a red light and broadsided her car at an intersection."

"When you were how old?"

"I was fourteen."

"And how long after that did your dad come here and start the school?"

"A year."

Ben's eyebrows arched. "So you'd just lost your mom and when you moved here and he became obsessed with this place it was like losing him, too."

"Actually, I guess it was. A little," Clair said. "I've never looked at it that way, but you're right. Thinking back on it, that is how it felt to me." And the fact that Ben had such insight was yet another thing about him that impressed her.

But even so she couldn't let him think unkindly of her father, so she said, "Not that my dad wasn't a great guy. He actually never neglected me or ever left any doubt that he loved me. He just… Well, I guess he just dealt with my mother's death the only way he could. And for him, that meant quitting his job as a high-school teacher and finding something that filled more of his time."

"So he taught high school before opening the school?"

"He did."

"Then why did he opt for making it a treatment facility for younger kids when his experience was with older ones?"

"That was because of me. He decided only to take kids from eight to twelve so I wouldn't be living and working in close proximity to boys my own age and older."

"For safety's sake to keep you away from someone who might be predatory or because he didn't want some hellion like me corrupting you?"

There was that hint of devilry again that gave his oh-so-handsome face just an added bit of sexy allure. But again Clair tried not to notice. Too much, anyway.

"Both reasons—so I wouldn't be in contact with someone who could do me harm and so he didn't end up with one of his charges as his son-in-law," she confirmed, thinking that if Ben had been around here when they were both sixteen or seventeen and turned on the charm, he just might have weakened her defenses that much earlier.

But she didn't want him to know what she was thinking and so she continued talking about the boys her father *had* accepted into his program.

"Even some of the really young kids were a handful, though. My dad paid me to work around here after school, and there were times, with certain kids, when things weren't pleasant."

"I'm sure that's an understatement," Ben said. "While I was doing my master's thesis I worked in a facility for kids even younger than your dad accepted here. I saw plenty that no one would expect from a small child. I had a five-year-old call a therapist a name that would have made a longshoreman blush and then slash her arm with a razor blade he had hidden in the sole of his shoe—something he'd learned from his big brother's time in jail."

"Wow," Clair said, duly amazed. "Dad didn't take any kids with a history of violence against other people, but he did have a few who could hurt themselves when they had a bad day."

Ben's mention of work and doing his master's thesis seemed like an opening for her to ask about his education and credentials—something she was curious about since owning the school didn't require anything more from him than that he hire the professionals he needed, and she didn't know what he'd done after high school graduation. So rather than continue trading war stories, she said, "You have your master's degree?"

"I have my bachelor's in psychology and my master's in counseling."

That made her smile.

"What?" he demanded, smiling, too, albeit with some confusion tingeing it. "You don't believe me?"

"Oh, I'm not doubting your word. I was just thinking that you were a long way from being the guy anyone in our senior class would have thought of as the person most likely to end up with a graduate degree."

He laughed. "Predictability was never what I was known for, no."

Which was also part of his appeal, part of what made him the bad boy in the first place. Certainly he'd taken her off guard that night at the reunion and led her to even surprise herself.

"I still don't know exactly what you do for a living," he said then. "Or how it is that you can take time off from it to be here."

"I run my own day-care center," she confessed. "And since I'm the boss and have a lot of comp time to get back, I left my assistant director in charge while I'm gone."

Pregnancy hormones had made Clair unusually tired and her strenuous day caught up with her all of a sudden, making her yawn without warning.

"Oh! Where did that come from?" she said after the fact, embarrassed.

Ben laughed but she wasn't sure whether it was at her yawn or at her embarrassment over it. "Looks like I wore you out today," he said then.

"Hey, I made it longer than Cassie did," she countered.

"Well, to be honest, you tried to cash it in when she did. I just didn't let you," he reminded. "But maybe I'd better let you go get some rest now so you'll be ready to introduce me to the food wholesaler and the laundry service rep tomorrow."

"Maybe you'd better," Clair agreed, knowing the pregnancy fatigue wasn't something she could ignore.

She stood and began to gather the paper plates and pizza boxes that still littered the coffee table but Ben put a halt to that.

"Leave it. I've abused you enough for one day. I'll toss all this after I get you home to bed."

Had he intended that to sound as suggestive as it had?

He must not have because he amended it, "Or at least after I get you out to the cottage."

But there was still an edge of mischief to his tone that told her that even though he might not have meant his original comment to be as suggestive as it had come out, he was more amused by his slip of the tongue than rattled by it the way she would have been if she'd said it.

"I mean it. Leave the mess," he repeated when she didn't immediately stop cleaning up. "Come on, I'll carry this box of stuff out for you."

He stood then, took her one-eared stuffed dog from its perch on the coffee table and handed it to her. "If you have to have something to keep your hands busy, carry this poor, abused animal while I take the box."

Clair didn't have any choice but to accept her toy as he picked up the box, but still she said, "That's not heavy. I can take it myself and save you the trip." Although tonight she liked the idea of having him walk her to her door.

For no reasons she wanted to analyze too closely.

But Ben wouldn't hear of her carrying the box herself. "It's the least I can do after how hard I worked you today—even if you did stand me up for breakfast."

"I'm sorry about that," she said, omitting the fact that he was partly responsible because thinking about him had been the cause of her not getting to sleep early enough the night before.

"Yeah, well, tomorrow it's nothing but dry toast, and I'm not doing that until you actually show up," he threatened with only mock sincerity.

"Tomorrow I'll be on time. Early, even. I swear," she said.

"Uh-huh," he retorted facetiously, as if he didn't believe her.

He led the way from the living room through the kitchen and out the sliding doors with Clair following behind.

Following behind and unable to keep her eyes off the intriguing juggling act going on behind the rear pockets of his jeans with the rise and fall of a derriere that was easily one of the best she'd ever seen.

Then they reached the cottage and she barely managed to raise her gaze before he caught her, veering around him to open the front door.

"I can take that stuff now," she said, replacing the toy dog she'd been holding tight to her chest and reaching for the box.

This time Ben gave it over to her and she expected

that once he had he would say a simple good-night, turn and go back to the house.

But instead he waited for her to cross the threshold and still he stayed standing just outside the door.

"I haven't told you how much I appreciate you coming here and helping the way you are," he said then.

"It's no big deal."

"It's a big deal to me. And a big help. And not something you had to do. And I want to say thanks."

Clair suddenly had a flash of memory that had eluded her before that moment. A flash of memory of Ben walking her to her room at the bed-and-breakfast when they'd left the reunion. Of him beginning to say good-night to her.

But kissing her instead.

And continuing to kiss her all the way into the room.

And despite the fact that the kiss itself wasn't vivid enough in her mind to recall any details, that flash was enough to stir some of the same feelings she'd had at the time.

Feelings that had made her *want* him to kiss her.

Feelings that made her *want* him to kiss her again right at that moment....

Which she didn't think he had any intention of doing and for a split second she couldn't remember what, exactly he *was* doing.

Until she forced herself to concentrate on what he was saying again just as he said, "So, thanks."

For coming back to Northbridge and helping him

with the school—that was what he was doing, he was thanking her.

"You're welcome," she finally said, as if her mind hadn't just drifted backward in time and into dangerous territory.

"Well, welcome or not, I still owe you big for this."

"No, you really don't," she assured him.

But Ben merely smiled so sweetly it erased all the hints of bad boy she'd seen lurking around the edges and said, "I really do."

For a moment he looked at her very intently and those thoughts of him kissing her flooded right back into her head.

But they still didn't seem to be in his because then he said, "I'll let you get some rest," and took a step backward. "Good night."

"Good night," Clair responded, closing the door almost too quickly.

But she couldn't help it because the image of that other good-night they'd begun to say was still haunting her.

And so was the feeling of wanting him to kiss her.

And that just wouldn't do.

Not when she wasn't sure whether she was back in Northbridge to let him know he was going to be a father.

Or back in Northbridge to help with the school and then disappear from his life forever without telling him at all.

Chapter Three

"What'll it be?" Clair muttered to herself late Wednesday afternoon as she looked over the clothes she'd laid out on the bed. "The unisex camp shirt and the loose cargo pants? Or the skintight tank top and the butt-hugging black slacks? Hmm..."

The day had been packed with meetings during which Clair had introduced Ben to the wholesalers her father had used for foodstuffs, supplies and linens. Accounts had been set up, orders hashed through and submitted and arrangements made for deliveries to begin.

Now that it was all accomplished and Clair was back in the cottage, she'd had a refresher shower and shampoo, and she needed to dress for a family dinner at the

Walker home. The dinner was for Ben and Cassie's older brother Ad and his new wife Kit, who had just returned from their honeymoon. But Clair was torn about what to wear.

She was also thinking a lot about the fact that not only had Ben invited her, he'd also insisted that she go. And made it clear that he genuinely *wanted* her to.

But that wasn't why she was excited for the evening to come, she thought as she stared at the two outfits she was trying to decide between.

Ben was the only member of the Walker family Clair hadn't gotten to know through her friendship with Cassie. He was the only one who wasn't there during the many times she'd visited or had a meal there or spent the night.

But since Clair had left Northbridge, she hadn't had contact with the rest of the family, either. Once she and Rob had left town, they hadn't returned. Rob's family had moved to California about that same time and because Clair and her father had originally come from Denver—and because that was where her mother had been laid to rest—her father had opted for visiting her rather than having her visit him. That way he could always spend some time at the cemetery.

Upon his own death, her father had left firm instructions that he was to be buried beside his wife without anyone in attendance but Clair and her husband. So even though she'd received many bouquets of flowers from people in Northbridge—including the Walkers—

it had been ten years since she'd last set eyes on any-one but Cassie, who had visited her in Denver or met her for a few girls-only vacations.

That made tonight's dinner the first time Clair was going to see the other members of the Walker family in ten years.

And so Clair told herself that looking forward to the evening and worrying about what she wore were only due to that fact. That they had nothing to do with Ben.

But still, as she stood there debating what to wear, it was Ben she had in mind.

And images of his eyes popping out of their sockets when he saw her.

Which was ultimately why she opted for the white body-hugging tank top that showed off her pregnancy-induced, almost-two-sizes-bigger bust and the black slacks that had garnered wolf whistles from construc-tion workers when she'd worn them last.

But just to make herself feel a little less like she was choosing that particular top and pants to wow Ben, she also decided to wear the peek-a-boo white shirt over the tank top as a bit of camouflage.

And because this was a family dinner, she reminded herself. Not an intimate dinner alone with Ben.

Although that would have been nice.

But an intimate dinner alone with Ben was *not* why she'd come to Northbridge. Besides helping with the school, she'd come to sort through things. To make a decision.

A big decision.

Clair put away the camp shirt and the cargo pants, realizing as she did that her water glass needed refilling—drinking more water than usual seemed to help the intermittent bouts of nausea that pregnancy was also causing.

She left her bedroom, passing the bathroom that separated her room from the one that had belonged to her father, and went through an archway into the living room. Then she headed to the small kitchen at the rear of the house.

The four rooms—five if the bathroom was counted— were all that made up the cottage. But it was a cozy bungalow, and Clair didn't mind being there again the way she'd been worried she might. It was actually kind of nice to be in a place that reminded her of her dad.

Well, for the most part. She did try not to think too much about what her father's reaction might be to her unplanned, unwed pregnancy if he were there to know about it.

When she couldn't avoid it, though, she knew what her father would say about her current dilemma. He would say that Ben had a right to know he was going to be a father. Which was part of what she was there to decide.

It wasn't something Clair *dis*agreed with. It was just that when it came to this baby, she felt sort of selfish.

She wasn't proud of that. She hated to admit it even to herself.

But in the past year she'd lost her father, her husband

and the home she'd built with Rob. She'd lost half of what they'd received as wedding gifts, half of everything they'd acquired during their marriage. Rob—being Rob—had competed for the friends they'd shared and because her father's death and divorce had piggybacked and left Clair emotionally reeling, she simply hadn't had the energy to woo those friends to her side—so she'd lost many of the people in her life, too. She'd lost the future she'd been planning on, the future she'd been so sure she would have. She'd even lost half of the goldfish she alone had nurtured for years because Rob had actually gone to court to battle for them, and the court had even divided those down the middle—three to Clair and three to Rob.

And she knew, that had she and Rob had children, those children and every minute of their lives would have been something she would have had to fight for. So she couldn't help feeling that as long as Ben didn't know that she was pregnant, this baby was hers alone—like a wonderful, secret little gift to help ease the pain of all those other losses.

Not just any gift, either. The one gift, the one thing she'd spent the last three years of her marriage trying to have. The one thing that had been her deepest heart's desire for as long as she could remember. The one thing that she knew she couldn't bear to lose any part of….

Clair took her refilled water glass back to the bedroom with her and, after setting the tumbler on the dresser, she returned to the bedside, took off her bathrobe and put on the tank top.

But as she pulled it down around her middle she paused to lay a palm to her abdomen. To that spot where her baby grew.

Her baby.

Hers alone…

She could almost hear her father's voice telling her that wasn't true. That the baby *wasn't* hers alone. But she pushed the thought away, convinced that, if no one else knew, it *was* hers alone.

Her baby.

That was the biggest, most important thing—that she was going to have a baby. The nausea didn't matter to her. The dizziness she occasionally suffered didn't matter. The fatigue. The need for more trips to the bathroom. It was all worth it. Anything she had to go through was worth it. Including her dilemma over Ben.

Yes, she'd been shocked when the doctor had told her she was pregnant. Shocked silly. Shocked right into a flat-out faint.

But when she'd come out of that faint, when the news had sunk in, when she'd actually realized that she was going to have a *baby?* Well, that was when it had felt like she'd been given a gift.

And it also didn't matter that that gift had been given during one night when too much liquor and a man with too much charm and charisma had caused her to throw caution to the wind—including when it came to using protection.

Clair gave a last gentle pat to her belly and then took her hand away, reaching for her slacks to put those on, too.

Her baby, she thought again, feeling very, very possessive. Very, very protective.

But then that wasn't really so difficult to understand, was it? She was finally going to have what she'd been afraid—terrified actually—that she would never be allowed at all. Of course she felt possessive and protective.

Plus, when it came to Ben, it wasn't *only* that letting him know about the baby, sharing the baby with him, felt like it had the potential for losing a portion of this most precious gift. There was also the fact that he was a stranger to her. That she didn't know if he wanted to be a father or what kind of father he would make or anything about him except that he'd been in enough trouble as a teenager to be sent away.

And that he still had enough high-voltage bad-boy sex appeal to get *her* in trouble.

So being in Northbridge to help with the school was, in a way, just a cover. A cover for getting to know Ben and what made him tick and what he wanted and what might happen if she did decide to share her secret with him. A cover while she figured out if she could bring herself to share her secret with him.

And getting to know Ben and what made him tick was what she would be doing again tonight when she would see him with the rest of his family. Which was good. It was better than an intimate dinner alone with him because it would give her the opportunity to see his interactions and relationships with the important people in his life.

Yet there she was, dressed in the sexy tank top and the butt-hugging slacks, she thought as she put on the blouse and took a look at herself in the cheval mirror in the corner of the bedroom.

"Probably the looser clothes would have been more appropriate," she lectured her reflection. Because after all, she was dressed more for a date than a family dinner.

But she refused to think of this as a date. She didn't want to date Ben or anyone else. She'd only been divorced for six months and she was aeons away from being ready to be involved with another man. In fact, she wasn't altogether sure that she would *ever* be ready for it. That she would ever be able to trust another man enough to let herself get involved. Not after what she'd just been through. After the disillusionment and what had seemed like the shattering of all her dreams in one single moment.

But that was the past, and she was trying hard not to dwell on it. To only deal with the here and now. To keep her wits about her and to not do anything stupid. Like anything that could lead to repeating that night with Ben at the reunion.

No, she was absolutely *not* going to let there be a repeat of *that* to cloud things any more than they already were.

And if tonight *were* a date it could be a prelude to repeating that night at the reunion or even a prelude to what had been on her mind the previous evening at the cottage door when she'd had that flash of memory of him kissing her.

And that urge to have him do it again.

So tonight was definitely not a date.

And dating and preludes to anything at all were definitely not what this trip to Northbridge was about.

But as she brushed her hair and fluffed the curls into place, she couldn't help wishing that there was a little less voltage in Ben's sex appeal.

Because as it was, in spite of her best intentions, it wasn't easy not to get just a little charged up by it.

Or even a lot charged up.

Rather than allow Ben to pick her up at the cottage, Clair had insisted that she just meet him at the main house after she'd changed her clothes and they could go from there.

So when she was ready, she crossed the short bricked path to slip into the kitchen through the sliding glass doors.

But rather than finding Ben there, she discovered a note on the island counter addressed to her, instructing her to come upstairs to the dorm rooms—he had something he wanted her to see.

There wasn't anything even the slightest lascivious about the note and yet what flashed through Clair's mind was hardly innocent when she wondered what he could possibly want to show her in the sleeping quarters.

By the time she reached the second floor, she caught

a whiff of Ben's cologne. He wore a scent that made her think of fresh sea breezes, and although it was only a subtle hint lingering in the air, she could tell that she was following in his footsteps. And it didn't make it any easier to combat those less-than-pure thoughts as she climbed the last of the steps that rose to the third floor.

The attic level had been turned into four open rooms that provided dormitory-style housing. When she reached that floor she said, "Ben? Are you up here?"

"I'm back in the big room," he called in response, his voice coming from the area farthest from the stairs.

Clair headed in that direction, trying to ignore the fact that she liked the deep, rich sound of his voice as much as she liked the way he smelled.

He didn't seem to be in the room he'd said he was in when she got there, though, so again she said, "Ben?"

"I'm in the closet."

"What are you doing?" she asked when she stepped into the walk-in closet to join him and saw that he was replacing baseboard that he'd removed.

"When I was in the Arizona Center this was a prime stashing place," he explained. "We pried off the baseboard, knocked holes in the wall behind it to stuff contraband into and then put the baseboard back so no one was the wiser."

"So you're checking to see if there are any hiding places down there," Clair said.

"That's what I'm doing."

"Are there?"

"I've found a couple of places. One with a really old chocolate bar in it."

"Is that what you wanted to show me?"

Ben was down on the floor and he grinned a sly grin up at her. "No, something else. Over there." He pointed to the opposite side of the closet. "It's on the underside of the shelf. I spotted it when I was pulling the baseboard below it."

Clair moved to where he'd indicated, bending over and contorting enough to look underneath the shelf.

Sean loves Clair was carved into the wood.

"Ahhh, I remember Sean," she said affectionately when she spotted it.

"Did you have a secret admirer or something going with this Sean guy?"

Clair stood up straight again and, with an exaggeratedly dreamy intonation, said, "Tall, dark, handsome, amazing blue—"

She stopped short when she realized she'd been about to say *blue-green* eyes and describe Ben rather than the imaginary man she'd been creating as a joke.

"—blue eyes and dimples in both cheeks," she finished belatedly, hoping to cover her tracks.

But Ben saw through her—at least enough to figure out it wasn't the real Sean she was describing. "Yeah, right. I'm betting Sean was eight years old, three feet two inches tall, with a cowlick and a crush."

Clair didn't attempt to go on with her jest but she did laugh and own up to the truth, grateful that it had escaped Ben that he'd been the model for her fantasy man. "Sean was nearly ten, from a rough neighborhood in south L.A., tough as nails, and I tutored him in reading my last two months here because he was so far behind."

"Did you know he loved you?" It was Ben's turn to pretend to be taking this very seriously.

"I had a hunch when he offered to be my escort to the prom."

"And you turned him down and broke his heart?" Ben accused as if, on behalf of all the Seans in the world, she'd wounded him, too.

"His bedtime was eight-thirty and the dance didn't start until nine—what else could I do?"

"And that night, while you were out with another man, poor Sean probably sneaked in here after lights-out and carved his message into the wood for all eternity," Ben concluded melodramatically.

Clair laughed again. "And now he's twenty and doesn't even remember I existed."

"Oh, I wouldn't be too sure about that. First love—unrequited… We tough guys hide it, but we don't get over that. Besides, you're pretty memorable," he added pointedly and with a hint of that wickedness he could let slide into his voice or his expression without warning.

"Uh-huh," Clair responded facetiously to let him know she didn't believe it for a minute.

He'd finished replacing the baseboard by then and he stood and gave her her first real glimpse of him.

He'd changed out of the slacks and dressy sports

shirt he'd worn to meet people today, and now he had on more casual clothes—jeans and a dark blue polo shirt that caressed his every muscle and made his eyes seem more blue than green. He was also freshly shaven—which accounted for the scent of his cologne—and suddenly that closet seemed awfully small to share with anyone who looked and smelled so good.

It all worked together to make Clair's stomach flutter. Which, she knew, couldn't be the baby because it was too early in her pregnancy to feel any movement. No, this flutter was caused solely by the baby's daddy.

"We should probably get going," she said, wondering if he could tell that her throat was tight.

If he could, he didn't let it show. He also didn't move out of the closet—or out of the path to the door.

Instead he took a long, slow glance at her and smiled again. "If Sean ever saw you looking like that he definitely hasn't forgotten you," he said, his tone full of appreciation and more of that wickedness that went right to her head.

"Thanks. I think."

"I kind of hate to share you."

"It's just Sean possessing you and telling you to keep me in this closet with his message," she joked feebly.

Ben pretended to consider that, using it as an excuse to go on giving her the once-over. "I don't think so," he concluded after a moment, the heat of his gaze making Clair's temperature rise.

But just when she was becoming aware of urges she didn't want to have—like the urge to lay her palms to those pectorals barely contained in that shirt, or to have more than his eyes traveling over her—he finally conceded and stepped out of the way of the door.

"You're right, we probably should get going or my mom will have my hide for keeping everyone waiting to eat."

Mention of his mother gave Clair a new opening and, good-naturedly mimicking the older woman, she said, "Dinner's at six-thirty. Not six-twenty-five. Not six-thirty-five. Six-thirty."

"So you know Lotty Walker's drill."

"I do. I've had dinner there a time or two in the past."

"Not when I was there."

"No, before you came back."

"And after that? You didn't want to dine with a delinquent or your dad wouldn't let you?"

"By then I was with Rob every waking moment."

Ben nodded sagely. "And on what sounds like a sour note, we'd better adjourn before our evening gets tainted."

"Good idea."

Ben motioned for Clair to go out ahead of him and she did, sensing his eyes once again on her the whole way and wondering if he liked the butt-hugging slacks as much as the construction workers had.

Not that it made any difference, she was quick to remind herself.

But when they reached the kitchen and Ben said, "I'll just wash my hands and we can leave," she thought his voice had a huskier quality to it.

And despite the fact that she knew it shouldn't be so satisfying to think the posterior view of her had accomplished that, it was.

The drive to the Walker family home took less than ten minutes in Ben's SUV—the average time required to reach almost anything in Northbridge.

The house was a redbrick, two-story, the upper level was only slightly smaller than the lower, and all the windows were trimmed with white shutters.

But it was the wide front porch that Clair stared at nostalgically as Ben parked at the curb. She remembered lazy summer afternoons when she and Cassie had lounged there, painting their nails, eating cookies, drinking iced tea and talking and talking and talking.

She was so lost in her memories that she didn't think to get out of the car even after Ben had stopped the engine and she was slightly surprised when he came around to open her door.

"Are you seeing ghosts dancing up there or something?" he asked, clearly noticing her preoccupation.

"I was just thinking that it looks the same," she said.

"It should look the same. Nothing much changes in Northbridge—it's part of the charm," he said as Clair finally stepped out onto the curb where a grass strip separated the street from the sidewalk before the rest of the lawn ambled up to the bushes that lined the front of the porch.

When they reached the big front door Ben didn't

knock or ring the doorbell. He just opened the screen and ushered Clair inside.

"Where is everybody?" he called then, since no one was in the living room they walked directly into.

"Kitchen!" someone shouted from the rear of the house.

Ben checked the clock above the mantel. "Oh-oh, six-thirty-three—we could be in trouble."

There weren't any signs of trouble when they reached the big, pastel country kitchen, though. A rousing round of hellos greeted them instead, and Clair was rushed with a slew of open arms all wanting to welcome her with a hug before Ad's new wife, Kit, was introduced to her.

Then Lotty Walker shouted, "Soup's on!" to announce the meal just as the older woman had announced every meal Clair had ever had in the Walker household.

Lotty took the seat at the head of the large oval table in lieu of the husband she'd lost twenty years ago, and Cassie assigned the rest of them chairs, putting Clair between her and Ben. And the moment everyone was seated platters of food began to make the rounds.

Dinner talk was lively in the process, allowing Clair to catch up on the family. In addition to what she already knew about Ben and Cassie, she learned that Ad still owned the restaurant and bar on Main Street that bore a variation of his name—it was called Adz. That Reid— the next-to-youngest Walker—had finished his training and returned to Northbridge to work in the local hospital as an emergency room physician. And that Luke, the baby of the family, was a police officer on the small local force.

For Clair the meal made her feel as if she'd come home, as if she were a part of the family.

But then that was how she'd felt all those years ago, too.

She'd been so lost when her father had moved her to Northbridge—her mother had only been dead a year, she'd been uprooted from her friends and the house she'd lived in all her life, and her father had been so preoccupied with the Northbridge School for Boys that she'd been left adrift in many respects.

Just when she'd needed it most, the Walker home had been an oasis for her. A warm, loving mother, Lotty Walker had treated Clair like one of her own children, and Ad, Reid and Luke had teased and taunted and tormented her as much as they had Cassie—making her feel a part of things that way, too.

So being with them all again tonight was like being back with the surrogate family that had provided more comfort and emotional sustenance than they would ever know.

It also reminded her that those people, that family, were what had made her want a family of her own so badly.

Something she would have now.

Thanks to Ben…

Honeymoon pictures of the Bahamas followed dinner and it was nearly eleven by the time the evening wrapped up.

As much as Clair had enjoyed herself and seeing all

the Walkers again, she wasn't sorry when it was over. It was nice to once again be in the quiet car after all the noise of the large, boisterous family gathering.

It was nice to be alone with Ben.

But she didn't want to consider that.

And in an attempt not to—and not to dwell too much on how good he looked in profile even in the dim dashboard light—she said, "I was curious about how things were between you and the rest of your family. If you were the outsider. What the dynamics were."

Ben took his eyes off the road to cast her a glance. "Why?" he asked, sounding confused.

She couldn't admit it was part of what was basically research on him, so instead she said, "I guess because you weren't around when I was so I never saw you with them all. I wasn't sure how you fit in. *If* you fit in with them after spending time away when you were young. And because I assumed—then at least—that you were different."

"I *was* different. I got into trouble. But is that a roundabout way of asking if there were hard feelings because of my misspent youth?"

He was smiling slightly so Clair knew she hadn't offended him. "Something like that, yes," she confirmed. Plus she was wondering what his misspent youth had entailed exactly and was fishing for a little information.

"I'll admit it was a little awkward when I first got back home," Ben said, not appearing to have any problems talking about this subject. "I didn't *feel* like I fit in for a while. But that didn't last long. They're my *family*—you get back into the groove of that pretty easily. At least with a family like mine. But, no, I didn't have hard feelings about being exiled to Arizona. I deserved what I got. Sort of."

"Sort of?"

"What I was sent away for was something I didn't do. But I'd done plenty before that, which is why no one believed I hadn't done what I was sent away for. So, it wasn't as if I was an innocent angel."

"Ah," she said even though that didn't explain anything or enlighten her in any way.

They'd arrived at the school by then, and she wasn't sure she was going to get to hear any more since Ben parked his SUV in front of the main house and they both got out.

But then he inclined his head toward the side of the house and said, "It's a beautiful night. How about if I walk you around to the cottage?"

"Okay," Clair said, hoping that, if he wasn't ending the evening just yet, it meant he was going to continue with what they'd been talking about.

She was pleased to get what she wanted as they set off at a leisurely pace and Ben said, "I was a difficult kid."

Clair knew from Cassie that Ben and Cassie had been eight years old when their father—who had been an automotive mechanic—had been working under a car that had fallen and killed him, so she said, "Did losing your dad when you were so young have anything to do with that?"

"Sure, it was a factor. My mom had to go to work for the first time in her life. I was on my own a lot. But I'd have probably been into mischief even if my dad had been around. I was just that kind of kid. I was right there with the biggest troublemakers in town, making trouble myself. First, it was the little stuff—throwing rocks or snowballs, pocketing candy I wasn't supposed to have—minor transgressions. But the older I got, the bigger the transgressions. I did a lot of drinking and smoking, I broke into an abandoned warehouse to party, I knocked down mailboxes with baseball bats, painted graffiti, turned on the water sprinklers during the homecoming game…"

From the corner of her eye Clair saw him shake his head in disbelief at his own bad behavior before he added, "You name it, I pretty much did it. Or tried it."

"But why were you sent to Arizona for was something you *didn't* do?"

They'd reached the cottage by then and at the door Ben leaned one shoulder against the frame, blocking the handle and apparently not interested in going inside. So Clair mirrored his stance, leaning her own shoulder against the opposite edge of the door frame.

"I was sent into placement in Arizona for stupidity basically," he said wryly. "Something I had no shortage of in those days, since I ditched more school than I went to."

Clair had left the porch light on and it rained a soft yellow glow down on them, illuminating Ben's handsome features as he finally answered her question about what, exactly, had gotten him to the Arizona Center for Adolescents.

"A friend picked me up in a brand-new sports car. He said his old man had just bought it and let him drive it for the night. My friend was older than I was. I was a week shy of my fifteenth birthday, but he'd already turned sixteen. We went out joyriding—first he drove, then I talked him into letting me have a turn. We went all the way to Billings. Driving so fast it's a good thing we didn't crash or neither of us would have lived through it. Anyway, we shot through Billings like race car drivers but somehow missed getting pulled over— luckily. Then we made it all the way back to North-bridge and got stopped on Main Street by the police chief. That was when I found out that my friend had lied about the car."

"He didn't have his dad's permission to take it," Clair guessed.

"Oh, much worse. The car wasn't his father's at all. It belonged to a neighbor, who had just picked it up at the dealer that afternoon. My friend had stolen the guy's brand-new sports car."

"But if you didn't know—"

Ben shook his head. "I was driving when we were stopped, which made me look pretty guilty. And with my reputation, nobody believed I hadn't been in on the whole deal. We were both charged with car theft and be-cause this is Northbridge, and everybody knew us, and because the judge took pity on my mom raising me alone, he gave our families the choice of sending us into private placement or putting us into the public system."

"Was the Arizona Center public or private?"

"Private. My mom had to borrow against the house to pay for it, but if she had let me go into the public system it would have been a lot worse in terms of the state becoming my guardian and the courts and social services being able to put me wherever there was an opening. My mom was too worried about what might happen to me under those circumstances, so she took out a second mortgage," he added quietly, clearly ashamed of that fact now.

"But it all worked out," Clair said. "So I'm sure she considered it worth it."

"Still, it wasn't something she should have had to do. And even though I paid the money back to her a year and a half ago, I still feel like dirt for putting her through what I put her through."

Clair could tell that was no exaggeration. "It couldn't have been much fun for you, either—having to leave your family and be in even a private placement facility," Clair said, unsure how to soothe his guilt for his youthful misdeeds but trying to find a way.

"It was anything *but* fun. It was more like three years and three months of hell. But that was the basic philosophy of that particular program," he said with an undertone of anger and resentment in his voice.

"And after three years and three months of hell you decided to make it your life's work?"

"It served its purpose—it straightened me out. But I didn't agree with the method. It was more like a prisoner of war camp than a school. We slept on mats on the floor. There was no privacy. No privileges. No way to *earn* privileges. No rewards. It was purely a toe-the-line-or-else system of miserable consequences for even the most minor infraction—like oversleeping so much as one minute. I just thought there were better ways to deal with us. Maybe not with some of the worst of us, but with most of us."

"And you decided to do that?"

"I decided to find out if it was possible. That's why I went to college to study psychology. It's why I got my master's degree. It's why I've worked in different placement situations since then—to learn all the methods, all the techniques. To learn if doing it the way I wanted to do it would work."

"Did you learn that?"

"I think so. But don't get me wrong. This isn't going to be a warm and fuzzy placement," he said with a nod in the direction of the main house. "My kids will be up early, they'll have chores and responsibilities, they'll have to participate in their own care and the care and maintenance of this place. They'll do community service in town, along with school and group counseling sessions and individual therapy. It'll be hard work—and plenty of it—and when their heads hit their pillows at night, they'll be ready for sleep. But they'll also be on a point system so everything they do every day will be evaluated, and when they've done what they're supposed to do, they'll earn levels that will bring privileges and rewards."

Clair could tell that he felt very strongly about this subject, that he knew exactly what he did and didn't want going on at the Northbridge School for Boys. And she admired that. From his own adversity, he'd devised a better plan for teenage boys headed down the wrong road. Even if the strength of his determination did remind her a little of things in her recent past that she was glad to have behind her.

"The way I see it," he continued, "these are kids who have screwed up—there's no sugarcoating that. But if every response to them is unreasonably negative, like it was in Arizona, well, negativity perpetuates negativity. It doesn't teach coping skills. It doesn't teach a better approach to handling whatever situation they were in that led to what they did. It doesn't open their eyes to how to make better, wiser choices, how to think things through and resist impulses or deal with anger issues—"

"And that's what you want to do."

"Those things, and I also want to show them other, more productive outlets to their energies and frustrations and angers. I want to give them the satisfaction of being rewarded when they *do* do something right so they start to see that that's preferable, that it's a whole lot better to get the strokes than the slams."

Clair couldn't help smiling at him, at the zeal and fervor that had grown in his voice the longer he'd talked about this. "Too bad you don't have stronger feelings on the subject," she teased.

That made him smile. "Now you know better than to get me started," he said with a sexy edge to his voice that insinuated passion for more than his chosen profession.

Passion she knew lurked just below the surface.

But *that* wasn't what she should be thinking about and so she returned to what had begun their conversation in the first place. "I'm just glad to see that you're back in the bosom of your family."

Not the best choice of phrases, she realized after it was said.

It opened the door for Ben to raise a cocky eyebrow, glance for only a split second at her bustline, and say, "Definitely a good place to be."

"Oh, I walked right into that, didn't I?"

"You really did," he agreed, looking no farther down than her eyes then, even though he was clearly enjoying the opportunity to tease her in return.

But as his gaze stayed on her eyes, Clair felt things between them change. The teasing seemed to evaporate and in its place only that sexy edge remained.

Enough of a sexy edge that for a moment, when Ben eased himself off the door frame in a way that brought him closer to her, Clair thought he might have done it on purpose. That he might be about to come closer still. That he might be about to take her into his arms. To kiss her...

But just when she was preparing for it, he seemed to

pull back again. He even took his hands from his front pockets and transferred them to his rear pockets to draw himself up straighter, putting that much more distance between them suddenly.

He turned his head, too, to glance at the main house rather than looking at her, and said, "You've probably had enough of the Walkers for one night."

She would never let him know how untrue that was. At least that she'd hardly had enough of one Walker in particular—him. So instead she agreed.

"It's pretty late and we have all the prep work to do tomorrow for the social service inspection the next day."

Ben nodded but he didn't make any move to go. He just continued to stay where he was, glancing back at her again with a new intensity in his eyes.

And as Clair watched him, studying the play of golden light on his heart-stoppingly handsome features, she wanted him to kiss her even though she kept telling herself it was out of the question.

But then he nodded a second time and said, "Yeah, I'd better let you go in."

He meant it because he stepped completely away from her and the door.

"Thanks again—for tonight," she said, hating that there was disappointment in her tone and hoping he didn't hear it.

Then she went inside without any more hesitation and denied herself a last glimpse of Ben before she closed the door.

Still the image of him was vivid in her mind's eye—tall and gorgeous and sexy....

But it was good that he hadn't kissed her, she told herself. It was good that she hadn't kissed him. Good that all she'd done was work toward her goal of getting to know him.

And she *had* gained some ground in that.

She'd learned about his childhood misdemeanors. About what had shaped him into the man he was now. About his vision and aims for the school he'd undertaken.

And that was all good.

It honestly was.

It was just that no matter how good it was, she couldn't help feeling that it somehow wasn't quite as satisfying as it would have been if he actually had kissed her.

Chapter Four

"Whoa! Are you all right?"

"I just need to sit down."

Talk about bad timing for a pregnancy-induced dizzy spell. It was late Thursday afternoon and Clair and Ben were together in the small confines of the closet that would function as the narcotics closet for any prescription drugs the school's charges might be on when Clair's head suddenly went light and she fell against one of the walls and had to slide to the floor.

As she did, Ben's attention went from the shelves to Clair and with quick reflexes, he reached one big hand to her arm to ease her descent. Then he hunkered down so he was very nearby to take a close look at her.

"Are you sick?" he asked, his deep voice filled with concern.

"No, I'm fine," Clair answered as the tiny space seemed to spin around her. "Just a little dizzy."

"A *little*," he repeated. "You're white as a sheet and you look bad."

Clair managed a weak smile. "Thanks a lot," she said facetiously.

But Ben wasn't allowing her to lighten the tone and continued studying her, his brows pulled together in a worried frown. "Do you feel like you're going to pass out?"

"No, it's okay. I just got dizzy," she repeated.

He released her arm and pressed his index and middle fingers to the inside of her wrist to take her pulse.

"Your heartbeat is faster than normal but not alarming."

Clair was reasonably sure that the increase in her heart rate had less to do with the dizzy spell and more to do with the fact that he was touching her, that his hand was big and strong and warm and setting off little butterflies to flutter all through her bloodstream. But she didn't say that.

And it didn't help when he gently pressed the back of his other hand to her forehead to test her temperature.

"You're not overheated or clammy," he concluded. "Do you have any shortness of breath? Pain?"

"No shortness of breath or pain. Even the dizziness is getting better," she said because it was true.

But Ben wasn't convinced. "I'll call Reid."

"No!" Clair said too emphatically, worried that any

medical contact with his brother might reveal her pregnancy.

But sounding hysterical wasn't going to aid her cause, so she forced calmness into her voice and said, "Really. I'm fine. It's just been a long day and I hardly had any lunch—"

"You didn't have *any* lunch—two bites of that sandwich and you pushed the dish away."

Clair didn't have morning sickness but she did occasionally have bouts of nausea and lunchtime today had brought on one of them. As a result she hadn't been able to get the ham sandwich down.

"I just do this sometimes when I don't eat," she told him, omitting the fact that that had only been the case since she'd been pregnant. "It's no big deal."

Except for the fact that it could expose her condition when she didn't want it exposed.

"I still think I should call Reid. He's at the hospital. We can just go there and have him check you over."

Exactly what she *didn't* want.

"You better not get this wound up whenever a kid sneezes or you're going to be in the emergency room every time you turn around," she said to cajole him out of his concern. "This is not a big enough deal to even talk to a doctor about. I know what it is, and I'm here to tell you that it's absolutely nothing." Which was what her obstetrician had assured her after examining her when she'd fainted in his office. Dizzy spells and fainting were simply side effects of the early stages of pregnancy for some women.

"So I've just worked you too hard the last few days," Ben surmised.

They had had a busy day today preparing for the state inspection scheduled for Friday. Besides the double-locked closet for narcotics, they'd had to make sure emergency numbers were posted in all staff offices; that the first-aid kits were in order; that all beds were equipped with the required mattress pads, sheets, blankets and pillows; that cleaning supplies were adequate for killing staph bacteria, e-coli and strep; that there was the correct ratio mixture of bleach and water for disinfecting surfaces that food would not come into contact with; that there were fire extinguishers in every room and labeled as such; that no fire exit was blocked; that all sharp knives were under lock and key; and that the entire facility would meet safety and cleanliness standards.

"I'm used to being busy—I chase kids all day, every day," she said, denying that he'd worked her too hard. Which was the case, it was just that she was accustomed to hectic days under normal circumstances. But the fatigue of pregnancy *had* left her dragging a bit. And being in Northbridge again, with Ben, and hiding the fact that she was pregnant, were not normal circumstances. Apparently everything had just caught up with her this afternoon.

But she still wasn't going to admit that. "I'm fine. I'm not even dizzy anymore, it's passed," she added.

"You're sure?"

"Who would know better than me?"

He gave her an intense stare for a moment longer, as

if to judge for himself. But in the end he must not have seen anything to make him doubt her word because he said, "Come on then, let's get you out of this closet."

He stood, leaving Clair with a view of thick, jean-clad legs before he bent over and offered her both his hands.

She knew it was a mistake to take them but she didn't have a choice. So she slipped her hands into his, feeling her pulse speed up all over again as he took hold of her and pulled her to her feet.

Once the dizzy spells passed, it was as if they'd never happened in the first place and that was how it was now. Clair felt perfectly fine.

"Steady?" he asked.

"Completely," she assured.

He must have only half believed her because he let one hand go but kept hold of the other, leading her out of the closet and into the kitchen where he had her sit on one of the benches at the table.

Only then did he release her hand, making her miss his touch when he did.

"Still okay?" he asked.

"Still okay."

He went to the refrigerator and poured a small glass of orange juice, bringing it to her. "Drink this," he ordered as if he were in charge.

"I'm not really a fan of orange juice," she said, wrinkling her nose.

"Drink it anyway or I'll pick you up and take you to the hospital to see Reid whether you like it or not."

His tone let her know he meant the threat so Clair accepted the juice and drank some of it.

Then she set the glass on the table and said, "Bully."

"You bet."

He propped a hip on the tabletop and perched nearby, studying her again. "No more work for today," he decreed. "We're as ready as we're going to be for that inspection—"

"What about double-checking everything tonight?"

"We're not doing it. We're trusting our first run-through, and we're getting out of here. I'm taking you to Ad's restaurant for dinner and maybe, if you're up to it afterward, we'll have a walk to get you some fresh air. And then it's early to bed for you so you get a good, solid night's sleep."

"You have it all worked out."

"It's either that or the emergency room," he threatened again, less seriously this time.

"No emergency room," she said firmly, accepting his other proposal by default.

His take-charge attitude also caused a bit of a flashback to that night at the reunion in June. As the evening had waned, the band had played more and more slow songs, and the dance floor had been less crowded. Less crowded enough for Clair to see her former husband dancing with his new wife—holding her close, whispering in her ear, kissing her.

Clair's spirits had plummeted all over again—a condition not helped by the fact that she had been very inebriated by then—and for no reason she'd understood, Ben had realized it. Of course she hadn't let him know the cause, but he'd insisted it was time to get out of there and he'd whisked her off.

He'd also managed to chase away that resurgence of doldrums and made her feel a whole lot of other, much nicer things by the time they'd reached her room.

Which, she thought now, might have been reason enough *not* to give in to his taking charge again.

But tonight he was only deciding where they would eat and the possibility of a walk afterward, she told herself. There wasn't anything chancy in either of those and so she gave herself permission to simply enjoy this side of him and let herself roll with it.

"I'll need to shower and change clothes before I can go out," she informed him.

"Me, too."

"Can we leave in an hour?"

He hesitated, then inclined his handsome head and said, "I'm thinking maybe I should come over to the cottage with you while you get ready and sit in the living room so I'll be close by if you black out in the shower or something."

"That's not going to happen," she said in a hurry, as the images of Ben carrying her naked from the bathroom and lying her on her bed caused feelings to erupt inside her that had nothing to do with her health.

"Honestly," she insisted with force, "I'm fine now. The juice has given me a new lease on life, and once the dizziness goes away it really is gone for good. I won't have any problem showering."

"Humor me. I'd feel better knowing I'm there just in case."

There—just a few feet away from her bathroom, her bedroom….

That seemed more fraught with peril in the form of temptation than the risk of falling in the shower.

"No, no, no," Clair countered. "You're making too big a deal out of this. You need to forget it ever happened."

Ben looked skeptical but she could tell he was giving in. Probably because anyone who could raise her voice the way she just had was clearly not ill.

"You're sure?"

"Positive."

And to prove she was fully recovered, she stood, held out her arms, raised one foot like a flamingo, and said, "See? I'm a rock."

"Or a lawn ornament," he said wryly.

Clair put down her arms and leg and did a little taking charge herself by heading in the direction of the sliding door rather than entertaining any further discussion on the matter.

"I'll be back in an hour," she said.

"Sixty-one minutes and I'm coming over there," he warned.

"I'll be back in fifty-nine," she said, rolling her eyes at him before she slipped out the door.

She hadn't been understating how she felt now, though, because she genuinely did feel better.

Probably better than she should have been feeling.

Especially when it occurred to her that while she might have been able to convince herself that dinner with his family the night before hadn't been a date, it was more of a stretch to believe what they were doing tonight wasn't.

Still, it was another step toward her goal of getting to know him, she told herself. And that made it okay.

As long as that was *all* she did with him.

Clair showered and changed into a white, sleeveless mock-turtleneck, a pair of khaki capri pants and sandals. Since her hair was so short now, she could wash it and still trust that it would air-dry in a matter of minutes, after which she finger-combed the wavy mass into place, and applied makeup.

"Fifty-four minutes and twenty seconds," she claimed when she returned to the kitchen and found Ben waiting for her.

"Twenty seconds?" he repeated dubiously. "You were counting the seconds?"

"The point is, I made it back in less than an hour and without any problems."

"Looking good, too," he said, letting his warm eyes travel from top to bottom to top again. Then his gaze stalled on her hair and he tilted his head.

"I've been debating about what I thought of your new haircut," he told her after a moment.

"I thought you just hadn't noticed."

"How could I not notice? I just wasn't sure about the change—I liked you the way you were."

And she liked hearing that.

But she tried not to be too pleased and said, "So what's the verdict? Do you hate it?"

"Actually," he said ruminatively, "the more I see of you, the more I like it. It doesn't hide your face the way the longer hair did. And the curls are nice—softer."

"So the verdict is…"

"The haircut's a good thing."

"Thanks," she said. Then, teasingly, she added, "I like yours, too."

But even though she was teasing him, that didn't mean she *didn't* like the way he looked, because she did. He'd dressed in better jeans than he'd had on to work, and a heather-gray polo shirt that didn't have an inch to spare over his broad shoulders, bulging pectorals and big biceps. Plus he was freshly shaven and smelled terrific, and even though it wasn't a dead giveaway, she could tell he'd washed his own hair because the sexy disarray was slightly different than it had been all day.

In fact, she realized that she liked the way he looked *too* much and changed the subject.

"I think skipping most of lunch today has caught up with me. I'm starving," she announced then.

"Need something to tide you over until we can get to the restaurant?"

"I think I can make it if we leave right now." Before

she spent too much more time standing there taking in the heady sight of him.

Ben motioned toward the front of the house. "Let's go then."

Ad's restaurant was in one of the storefronts on Main Street. Fashioned like an old English pub, it sported dark green café curtains blocking only the lower half of the windows that faced the sidewalk and the doorway was in a small, recessed alcove.

Inside, a long, carved walnut bar was the focal point of the place, complete with a brass foot rail adorning the front of it and a full mirror behind it.

Free-standing tables took up the center floor, with leather upholstered booths lining the walls, and the food smelled wonderful.

Ben and Clair arrived at the height of the dinner rush so all the tables and booths were filled and several customers waited at the door. The hostess knew Ben, and after greeting him, told him his brother wasn't working tonight and that she could only put Ben's name on the list.

"I know, I should have called and let you know I was coming," Ben said. "But it's okay. We're not in a hurry. We'll wait at the bar."

Having said that, he placed a hand at the small of Clair's back to urge her in that direction.

It was odd how ultra-aware she was of something so small. But she was. And even though she cautioned herself not to be, she couldn't seem to help it. Any more than she could help regretting it when they reached a vacant spot at the bar and he took his hand away.

"What will you have?" he asked. "A margarita?"

The drink of choice at the reunion. The drink that had led to what had happened that night...

Clair doubted she'd have tempted fate by drinking that again even if she *could* have had liquor.

"I'll just have lemonade, thanks," she said.

"You don't want a glass of wine or a beer?" he suggested.

"No, just lemonade," she repeated, thinking that to her, the refusal of alcohol and the dizzy spell in conjunction with each other were revealing. But all she could do was hope that wasn't true for Ben.

He didn't seem at all suspicious as he turned to the bartender and ordered Clair's lemonade and a dark ale for himself, and instead came to another conclusion.

"Booze probably wouldn't be the best idea after nearly passing out this afternoon."

"Right," Clair pretended to confirm.

Within minutes of being served their drinks the hostess approached them to say that a table for two had opened up and since the other parties waiting were all larger than that, Ben and Clair could have it.

Then she led them to a small round table in a corner of the restaurant.

But being out of the line of traffic didn't offer any kind of privacy because once they were seated it seemed to be open season on them as people began to make a point of coming over to talk.

It was an element of small-town life that Clair had forgotten about. But in Northbridge, where nearly everyone knew nearly everyone else and everyone else's business, it was unheard of not to say hello. Plus, Ben being on the verge of launching a new endeavor, and this being the first time many people had seen Clair since she'd left town at eighteen, made for a constant stream of visits.

In between well-wishers Ben did make sure that Clair ate most of her salad, her pulled-pork barbecue sandwich, and her French fries, so that by the time they were finished she was very full and eager for a stroll along Main Street to walk some of it off.

"So tell me what's changed," she suggested as they began their stroll.

Ben laughed. "Not much."

He was right. Main Street itself looked the same as it had ten years ago when Clair had left Northbridge.

Most of the buildings were two or three stories tall, each one sharing the side walls of the next. They were old-fashioned, primarily brick buildings, each one lending a country-town feel in their own way—whether through the shop awnings and overhangs that reached out above the bricked sidewalk; or in arches and cornices and gingerbread eaves. Then, too, the tall, ornate wrought-iron pole lamps circled with flower boxes contributed their own charm all up and down Main Street.

As they walked, Ben filled Clair in on what *had* changed in Northbridge—businesses and shops that had been sold or handed off to relatives, new goods or services that had been added to keep competitive, who was doing rip-roaring business and who wasn't.

Then they approached the largest building on Main Street—the four-story, redbrick, former-mercantile-turned medical facility and five-room hospital that occupied the corner of Main and Marshall. And his tour guide impression stopped so he could poke his chin toward that.

"Here we are. And Reid's just inside. We could go in, let him take a quick look at you just to make sure everything's okay."

"Or we could keep going because there's not a single reason for a doctor to take a look at me," Clair countered.

"It would make *me* feel better."

"But I already feel better so there's no point. Surely after just paying for that meal I ate you can't think I'm under the weather," Clair reasoned.

"You want us to just walk by? To not even go in and say hello to poor, hardworking Reid?"

Clair laughed. "I'm not falling for guilt. Yes, I want to just walk by without even saying hello. At least that's what I intend to do because I'm sure that if I went in there to say hello to Reid you'd pull something to get him to examine me. But if you want to go in, I'll wait for you out here."

"You're a hard woman to help."

"I don't need help. I'm fine."

Ben took a deep breath and sighed. "I don't suppose I can drag you in kicking and screaming," he conceded.

"And that's what I'd do, too—I'd kick and scream. And don't think I couldn't throw the tantrum to end all tantrums because I've had some phenomenal fits demonstrated for me and at any moment I can call upon the worst of the worst of them to use myself."

That made him laugh, but he conceded to her refusal to go into the emergency room by continuing with their walk. "I'll bet you *have* seen plenty of tantrums since you run a day care and aren't an undercover operative for the CIA the way you said you were at the reunion."

Clair had forgotten the running joke that they'd maintained that night and the reminder made her laugh this time. "The day-care center could just be my cover, you know."

"Or it could be you're just a big fat liar."

She grinned but admitted nothing. "And you aren't a professional hit man—don't think I forgot that that's what you told me," she said, recalling his lie as they crossed Main Street to head back up the opposite side of it.

"Confess—a part of you believed me that night. You figured anything was possible of Cassie's delinquent brother."

"Well, if you were bad enough to turn on the sprinklers during the homecoming game, you were bad enough to do anything," she admitted.

"True," he agreed. "*Nothing* is as bad as that."

They'd made a full circle by then and reached Ben's SUV where it was parked at the curb in front of his brother's restaurant so he opened the passenger door for her, and Clair got in.

Then she watched him round the front of the vehicle, trying to ignore the sense that had come with this evening that something seemed to click whenever they were together. Something that involved more than merely the sight of his to-die-for good looks and that body that just wouldn't quit.

"Tell me about the day care," he said when he'd gotten behind the wheel, turned on the engine and pulled out behind the sole car coming down Main Street. "Are you working with kids of the rich and famous? Yuppie-puppies? Mean and rotten ones like I was?"

"Mean and rotten?" she repeated with a sideways glance at him.

"The phrase was used once or twice."

"That's awful."

"You might not think so if it was your mailbox I'd just smashed. But we aren't talking about me. We're talking about you and your kids."

Her kids—that was how she thought of them and it made her smile to think that he recognized that.

"No kids of the rich and famous, and I'm not sure what yuppie-puppies are. But we have a sort of even mix. Some parents are paying tuition and fees, some have to use other funding."

"Some advantaged and some disadvantaged," he

summarized. "Are they kids in trouble or just kids needing to be looked after while their folks work?"

"They aren't kids in trouble, I leave that to guys like you and my dad before you. But we try to do more than just warehouse our kids while their parents are at work. We can't do much more than cuddle and play with the babies but even with the toddlers, we make their days as constructive as possible. We teach them wherever we can, and our three-and-a-half-year-olds get started on some pre-preschool skills. Plus we offer a full preschool, and we have a good reputation for our kids excelling in kindergarten with what they've learned with us."

Ben was smiling again. "You're proud of it."

Okay, maybe she'd gone a little overboard in her answer to a simple question. "I am," she confessed.

"And you're the director of the whole place?"

"I am," she repeated. "I started there right after college as an aid and worked my way up. Now I run the whole place—from the nursery where we take six-week-olds all the way through the preschool that accepts even kids who aren't in the day-care portion, for which we have a waiting list."

"And you like it."

He wasn't asking. Apparently he could tell that she liked her job just from the way she talked about it.

"I love it. I wouldn't want to do anything else."

Except maybe stay at home with her own child.

They were back at the school by then and tonight Ben

pulled his SUV around to the rear of the house, parking next to Clair's car near the cottage.

She didn't know why he'd chosen to do that rather than park in front of the main house tonight, and she could have asked, but her thoughts were centered more on her own feelings about it.

Not that she cared where he parked. It was just that by parking so close to the cottage it seemed clear that the evening was ending, that they would get out of the car and go their separate ways from there. And although that shouldn't have been a big deal, she wasn't happy with the prospect when she still felt the urge to be with him.

It was probably the pregnancy, she told herself. It was probably just some kind of primal inclination to be with the father of her baby. Which was probably why babies were better born to married—or at least committed—couples.

But that wasn't how it was for her and the father of her baby. It wasn't even how she wanted it to be, she reminded herself.

So again she tried to ignore what she was feeling and simply got out of the SUV before Ben could make it around to her side.

She was right about this being the end of the evening, though, because he didn't invite her to the main house for a nightcap, he merely headed for the cottage then, walking her to her door.

Of course *she* could have asked *him* in to the cottage for a nightcap. But so far the evening had stayed per-

fectly within the parameters she'd assigned for this
visit—even if tonight had seemed like a date—and she
knew it was best to leave it at that.

"You're sure you don't want me to be here with you
for the inspection tomorrow?" she asked as she unlocked the door and reached in to turn on the light, remaining on the small front stoop with him.

"Nah, this is my baby, I'll handle it."

For a fraction of an instant she thought he was referring to the baby she was carrying—the baby that really
was his—before she realized that wasn't the case and
pulled herself out of the flash of panic that had accom-
panied the thought that he knew she was pregnant.

"Cassie would shoot me if I tied you up again, anyway," he continued. "She says she wants you all to herself at least one day, and since I've kept you working
every other day that you've been here—and since you're
leaving on Saturday—she gets tomorrow. Or else."

"Still—"

"Besides, after working you into a swoon today, I
think I have to let you off the hook."

Except that the more Clair thought about it, the more
she knew it was a hook she didn't want to be let off of.
Especially when Saturday and leaving Northbridge
were closing in on her, and she certainly wasn't any
nearer to any kind of resolution about what to do in regard to Ben and the baby.

But the plans had been made for her to spend Friday
with Cassie while Ben met with social services for the

inspection, and there was nothing she could do about it if he wanted to stick to the program.

"You're sure," she said.

"I'm sure. Hopefully, we'll have something to celebrate tomorrow night. I might even cook for you," he said with a slight wiggle of his eyebrows that almost looked nefarious.

Then his expression sobered somewhat and so did his tone as he seemed to be looking more intently at her suddenly.

"All kidding aside, are you all right?" he asked then.

"All kidding aside," she answered without hesitation. "I'm fine. Today's *swoon* was just a fluke. Low blood sugar from not eating, nothing else."

He nodded, keeping his eyes on her the whole while, again as if he were judging for himself.

But after a moment he altered his gaze slightly and smiled. She thought he'd probably been smiling like that just before he'd turned on the sprinklers at the homecoming game. Then he reached a hand to the back of her head, fingering the curls there.

"I really do like your hair. It makes me want to ruffle it up."

He didn't ruffle it up, though. Instead what he did was more a caress.

A caress that altered something in the air around them. Something that took hold of them both, that wrapped them in the moment alone as his smoky gaze seemed to bathe her and his hand suddenly cradled her head.

His lips parted, and it was the only warning she had before he leaned toward her and pressed them to hers. So softly it was a whisper that almost didn't touch her. So briefly it was over almost before it had begun. So chastely it was certainly nothing like any she could remember them sharing that night at the reunion.

But in a way that was nice. Sweet.

This kiss erased some of that other night when they'd rushed too swiftly to intimacy. It put them back where they should have been in the first place—at the beginning, when everything was new and so was whatever it was that was happening between them.

After the kiss he went back to looking at her, searching her face, her eyes.

But he didn't say anything about that kiss. He didn't apologize or make any excuses for it.

He merely smiled again. This one pleased. Happy that he'd done what he'd done, right or wrong.

Then he said, "Wish me luck tomorrow."

"Good luck tomorrow," she said.

"Have a good time with Cassie."

"I will."

One more kiss—only a peck just like the first—and he turned and left.

And even as Clair watched him go she still wasn't sure what those nearly infinitesimal kisses had been about.

But she was sure that she'd liked them…and the man who went with them.

Chapter Five

"I have a bone to pick with you," Ben said to his sister when Cassie stopped in to see him before going to the cottage to get Clair on Friday.

It was the first time he'd been alone with Cassie since finding out that Clair was newly divorced, and he stopped the paperwork he was doing at his desk to give his sister the hard stare as she sat in the visitor's chair across from him.

"What kind of a greeting is that?" Cassie chastised. "I come in to say hello and wish you luck on the inspection this afternoon and all you can say is that you have *a bone to pick* with me?" Cassie lowered her voice to mimic his words, clearly not taking him too seriously.

Ben continued anyway, in a peeved tone. "Why didn't you tell me why you wanted me to keep Clair occupied at the reunion?"

Cassie's eyebrows rose in question. "*Why* I wanted you to keep Clair occupied?" she parroted. "I wanted you to keep Clair occupied because I had to do some things, that's *why*. What else was I supposed to tell you?"

"That she needed company because she'd just gotten a divorce and her ex was there and she was miserable."

For the first time since she'd come in, Cassie looked like she was beginning to understand what he was talking about. "I didn't think it was my place to tell you about her divorce or her ex-husband. I figured if she wanted you to know her private, personal business, she'd tell you herself. *Did* she tell you herself?" Cassie challenged.

"Not until the other night."

"So apparently I was right *not* to tell you at the reunion," Cassie concluded victoriously.

"She thought you *had* told me at the reunion," Ben countered, trumping her in their sibling bickering match.

But Cassie was undaunted. She gave him a negligent shrug. "Well, now you know. She's divorced—"

"*Newly* divorced," Ben corrected pointedly.

"Yes, Clair is *newly* divorced. So what?"

"So you know how I feel about that."

"You feel like it's a mistake to get involved with a woman who's on the rebound because you got burned that way. What does that have to do with Clair?"

"You set me up with her."

Cassie looked shocked. "I did not!"

Ben pushed his chair back onto its rear legs and squinted his eyes suspiciously at his sister from down his nose. "Right," he said dismissively.

"I did not set you up with Clair. I wouldn't do that to you after what you went through with Heather. I know better."

"Right," Ben repeated. "Then what was that whole thing at the reunion?"

"Exactly what I said it was—Clair's my friend. I talked her into coming. She didn't think her ex would be there, so she agreed to come. He showed up with his new wife, she wanted to leave, I convinced her to stay and then couldn't stick as close-by as I'd promised her I would. So I asked you to *keep her company*—" Cassie enunciated those last words slowly and emphatically. "I was *not* setting you up."

Ben just went on staring at his sister, wondering if she was telling him the truth or hiding her own plot to get him together with Clair.

"Swear on Pinky's grave," he challenged with an old dare they'd used as children—Pinky was a rabbit they'd shared.

"I swear on Pinky's grave," Cassie said without hesitation. Then she laughed and made a face. "Why did we ever start that—swearing on Pinky's grave?"

"He was pure white except for his little pink nose and he was everything good—his purity and goodness couldn't be soiled with lies," Ben reminded her of the tradition begun when they were eight years old.

"Well, I swear on Pinky's grave that I was not setting you up with Clair. I wouldn't do that to either of you."

It was Ben's turn to raise his eyebrows. "Are you saying that setting her up with me would be bad for her?"

"No. But I already told you why I wouldn't set you up with her, and I wouldn't set her up with you because she's fresh out of a marriage and probably not ready for that. If this was two years from now and she was all healed and over her divorce—"

"And had already had a rebound guy or two—"

"And had already had a rebound guy or two. But not when she still has divorce-dust all over her."

Ben considered that. And the fact that his sister was not only an honest person but also that he'd never known her to do anything that might put him in jeopardy.

"All right then," he conceded after a moment. "But if I find out you're lying, the destruction of Pinky's purity is on your head."

Cassie didn't appear to be relieved because she'd never seemed upset—the sign of a clear conscience. She did, however, look as if her interest had been piqued.

"So, Clair really didn't tell you that night at the reunion that she was divorced or what was going on?" Cassie asked then.

"It wasn't what you'd call a getting-to-know-each-other evening. If you'll remember, I had to ask you what she did for a living because she told me she worked for the CIA—"

"And you told her you were a hit man. I remember," Cassie said.

"Right. That's what we did—we drank and joked around and just had a good time." But he still had no intention of telling his sister just *how* good a time they'd had.

"Then you didn't know about the divorce until now?"

"I don't know any of the details about it even now. All she told me is that the ex was at the reunion with his new wife and he wasn't supposed to be and she's new to the whole divorce thing so it upset her that night and caused her to behave unlike herself."

That sparked still more of Cassie's interest. More than he wished it had. "What do you mean she behaved unlike herself?"

"Just that she didn't feel like mingling and making small talk with everyone," he said, hoping his sister would accept his dodge.

She paused long enough to make him wonder but she didn't push the issue. "But she still hasn't given you all the gory details?"

"No." It was Ben's turn to pause as his own curiosity was spurred. "But there *are* gory details, huh?" he said.

"I'm not telling," Cassie insisted. "It's not my place now any more than it was at the reunion. If she wants you to know about it, she'll have to tell you herself."

Ben shrugged. "Okay," he said as if he didn't care after all. When he really did.

"Why should it matter, anyway?" Cassie challenged. "Why should anything about her divorce matter or whether or not you knew she was newly divorced? Unless…" Cassie let her voice drift off into suspicion.

His sister was turning the tables on him and he knew it. "It doesn't matter," he claimed aloofly.

"It mattered enough for you to want to pick a bone with me. You were ticked off that I hadn't told you she was just out of a divorce. And why would it tick you off not to be told that unless you *like* Clair?"

"I like Clair just fine," Ben admitted, putting an entirely different inflection on the word than his twin had.

"Maybe you more than like her—as in, maybe you have a little something-something for her?"

"And maybe you're a pain in my neck," he said as if this turn the conversation had taken was nothing more than that. Certainly nothing with any substance to it.

But it didn't throw Cassie off the track. She suddenly looked as if a light had dawned for her. "Is that why you got her back here to help with the school? Because you hit it off with her at the reunion—without knowing she'd just gotten divorced—and you wanted to see her again?"

"A gigantic, enormous pain in my neck," was Ben's only response.

"I'll bet it is."

But his sister sounded too gleeful for him not to defend himself. "I took Clair up on the offer she made to help get the school turned over to the new owner—*whoever* the new owner was—because I want this done right. It didn't have anything to do with that night at the reunion."

"*That night at the reunion*," she repeated. "Why does that make it sound like it was more than I thought it was before?"

He was getting himself in deeper and deeper. "You're imagining things," he said, working to keep his tone neutral.

"What happened *that night at the reunion* that I don't know about?"

"Nothing."

"Is that why the two of you disappeared without even telling me you were leaving? Was there something going on between you? Did you *hook up?*"

"Don't get carried away, Cassie," Ben said, shaking his head as if he couldn't believe where her imagination was leading her. "What happened that night at the reunion was that I did what you asked me to do. I kept Clair company, we joked around, and that was it."

"I don't believe you. I didn't think twice about a lot of things before, but now…"

Ben let his chair fall to all four legs again with a resounding thud. "Now nothing," he said, trying not to sound surly. And failing.

"You're attracted to her. Interested in her." Cassie paused as her thoughts obviously raced. "Or are you *involved* with her?"

"Don't you have somewhere else to be?" Ben asked as if she really were causing him pain.

"Something's going on. You can't fool me."

Once again he shook his head, thinking that anything—and apparently everything—he said only made this worse.

"Tell me," Cassie demanded.

"There isn't anything to tell."

"I'm pretty sure there is."

"Well you're wrong."

"Do I have to grill Clair?" she threatened.

"Only if you want to sound like a lunatic," he said, knowing that any attempt to prevent her outright would be adding fuel to the fire. "But if you *do* want to sound like a lunatic, by all means, go ahead."

"Does she know?"

"Does she know what?"

"That you *like* her."

Ben propped his elbows on his desktop and dropped his head into his hands. "You are sooo driving me crazy," he said to his chest.

"Do you want me to find out if she likes you, too?"

"Are we in second grade?"

"It might work out, you know?" Cassie said encouragingly and with excitement of her own echoing in her voice.

Ben sighed and looked up at her again. "I swear to you on Pinky's grave that there's nothing *to* work out."

Okay, he felt a little guilty for that because it might not be *completely* true. Not when he factored in those two tiny kisses that had ended the previous evening.

But they *had* been *tiny* kisses. Incredibly tiny indulgences on an impulse he'd had. An impulse he'd had since the moment he'd set eyes on Clair again.

Still, that didn't mean he wanted his sister knowing about it. Or knowing about what had happened the night of the reunion.

Or knowing that he was interested in Clair, which he damn well wished he wasn't.

In fact, he desperately didn't want his sister knowing any of that. Because it seemed like, if Cassie knew, the situation might get all the more out of control than it already seemed to be. And he was fighting like mad to *gain* some control over it. Over everything that every glance at Clair, every minute with Clair, every aspect of Clair seemed to raise in him. And desperate times called for desperate measure. Like swearing on Pinky's grave when he wasn't being completely honest.

"I wouldn't be rebound guy again for anyone," he said then, firmly, solemnly, in response to his sister's comment that things could work out between him and Clair.

"Maybe this time you wouldn't be rebound guy. Maybe this time you'd be the keeper," Cassie persisted.

"And maybe I have so much on my hands already with the school opening that I don't even have time to consider that. So don't get carried away. I just thought you should have told me what was really going on at the reunion."

He also thought that he'd managed pretty handily to bring this conversation full circle and hopefully knock the wind out of his sister's suspicions.

But his hopes were for naught because Cassie just smiled at him and said, "This could all work out nicely."

As far as Ben was concerned the only thing that worked out for him was that his phone rang just then, offering him an escape from what he'd gotten himself into.

"I'll let you get that," Cassie said, standing. "Besides, now I'm all the more anxious to spend today with Clair."

Ben shook his head and reached for the phone.

But even as he answered it and watched his sister leave his office he knew that it shouldn't have come as a surprise that Cassie had guessed something was going on between him and Clair.

Because something *was* going on.

He just didn't know what it was.

"This has been fun today. I'm so glad we got to do it," Clair told Cassie as her friend drove her back to the Northbridge School for Boys late that afternoon.

They'd had a long, lazy lunch. They'd browsed through Main Street's antique stores, boutiques and specialty shops. They'd strolled the college campus and Cassie had shown Clair her office. Then they'd stopped in at the campus coffee shop for chai teas and a scone to end their day together.

"I'm glad we got to do it, too," Cassie said. "But you haven't hated it *too* much that you've had to spend more time with Ben than with me since you got to town, have you?"

Clair didn't know why, but she had the impression that her friend was headed somewhere with that last question.

"No, I haven't hated seeing Ben," she answered, thinking that, in fact, even though she'd had a wonderful time with Cassie today, she'd missed Ben. Although she didn't want to acknowledge that even to herself.

"Am I mistaken or have you two hit it off a little?" Cassie asked, sounding as if she were tiptoeing around the subject and leading Clair to assume that was where Cassie had been headed in the first place.

"I don't know about hitting it off," Clair hedged. She'd been hoping that her friend hadn't picked up on any of whatever it was that seemed to simmer around her and Ben whenever they were in the same room. But even if Cassie *had* sensed something, Clair wasn't going to admit it.

"Oh-oh. Does that mean you *dislike* him?" Cassie asked, going to the other extreme.

"No, it doesn't mean I *dislike* him!" That had come out too quick and too forcefully not to sound odd. "I mean, of course I like Ben," Clair amended. "He's your brother. I like all your brothers."

"Then you *do* like Ben," Cassie persisted.

Clair shrugged negligently. "He seems to have gotten his act—and himself—together again after his teenage foray into rebellion. I'm happy for him. And for your mom and the rest of you. I know everything that went on with him was rough on your family." More hedging.

"Ben has gone a whole lot further than just getting his act together. He's great."

Clair smiled and glanced at her friend. "Are we just slightly proud of our brother?"

"Yes. But there's so much to be proud of. Ben turned himself and his entire life around. He went to college—all the way to getting his master's degree. He works hard. He's already helped countless kids. He paid back my mom every penny it cost her to put him in that place in Arizona when he got in trouble. He took that experience and learned from it and formed a better plan for treatment than what he went through, and now he's opening a facility of his own—"

"If he ever decides to run for the Senate you should be his campaign manager and do his commercials," Clair commented with yet another laugh at her friend's enthusiasm. "But why does this sound like a sales pitch now?"

"I'm just saying he's a great guy," Cassie said.

"Okay. Ben's a great guy. You'll get no argument from me."

"So if the two of you have hit it off—"

"Ah." Light was dawning for Clair.

Cassie continued. "You're great. He's great. It would be…great."

Clair laughed yet again.

"*Have* you hit it off?" Cassie asked with a sideways glance at her.

"Cassie…" Clair moaned.

"I know, you just got divorced and you aren't ready."

"That's so much of an understatement you'll never know…"

Cassie took her eyes off the road to cast her a sympathetic glance. "I know it was rough with Rob."

"Earth-shattering for me," Clair corrected.

"But now it's over and you have to move on."

"That doesn't necessarily mean that I'm going to move on to another man."

"That doesn't sound like the Clair I know and love," Cassie cajoled.

"I don't think I *am* the same Clair I was before."

"Of course you are," Cassie insisted.

"No, I don't think I am, Cassie. The whole Rob-thing rocked me. It changed me."

"How?" Cassie asked dubiously.

"The biggest way is that every time I so much as imagine getting involved with anyone again I do a sort of mental recoil. I feel like I need to play turtle—pull all my vulnerable parts inside to keep them safe. It's as if I've lost the ability to trust a man as far as I could throw one. Any man. *Every* man. It's so bad that last week one of my preschool teachers got engaged and instead of being happy for her, I actually almost lost it and told her not to do it—even though I've never even met her fiancé."

Cassie flinched at that and made a pained face.

"I know, it's horrible," Clair conceded. "But that's what went through my mind and I had to use all of my strength to keep my mouth shut. I couldn't bring myself to congratulate her. Luckily everyone else was and I just stood in the background forcing a smile."

"Wow," Cassie breathed in reaction to what had ended up almost a diatribe.

"I know," Clair said again, more quietly, surprised herself by how carried away she could get on the subject. "It's baggage, I guess. Or some kind of wound."

"Like breaking your leg falling off a horse—you're really terrified of getting back on the horse."

"That metaphor never had quite as much meaning for me as it does now," Clair agreed.

"But you know the saying?"

"That you have to get back on the horse," Clair supplied. "Or maybe you just have to stay away from horses forever."

"Well, horses are one thing," Cassie said with another laugh that eased some of the tension in the car. "But men? Do you really want to stay away from men forever?"

"Maybe," Clair said seriously.

"You might mean that right now, but *forever?* Really?"

"Maybe," Clair repeated because she believed it was true. At least it was true for a large part of her.

There was, however, also a small part of her for which that obviously wasn't quite the case, since she had Ben on the brain almost all the time lately, and she'd been none too sorry that he'd kissed her the night before.

But still, thinking about him and kissing him weren't the same as being involved with him. They weren't the same as opening herself up to him. They weren't the same as trusting him. And those were the things that that large part of her felt incapable of doing.

Cassie turned onto the drive that led to the school and up ahead they could see Ben taking grocery sacks from the passenger seat of his SUV.

"For what it's worth," Cassie said then, her enthusiasm for this subject clearly weakening, "Ben really is a great guy."

But even great guys had their own agendas, their own baggage, their own tempers and weaknesses and wants and desires, Clair thought. And what if somewhere in those aspects of Ben there was the need or the desire to raise their child himself—the way he'd been determined to open his own placement facility so he could deal with troubled kids using methods he believed should be used? What if somewhere in those aspects of Ben there was the same kind of drive Rob had had to take everything for himself and leave her with as close to nothing as he could? Then Ben might sue for custody. And if he won? He could take away her baby.

"I'm sure Ben is a great guy," she said in response to his sister's comment. "But I just don't think I can put it to the test."

"Right now, anyway," Cassie added again.

This time Clair didn't refute it the way she had moments earlier.

But she still thought, *or maybe ever…*

* * *

As Clair changed clothes for the dinner Ben was preparing to celebrate having passed his social services inspection and being certified to reopen the facility, it struck her how fast this trip had come to an end. She'd arrived on Monday evening and was scheduled to leave in the morning.

Originally, that had seemed like a long time. A week of close contact with Ben when she was embarrassed about what had happened at the reunion. When she was carrying his baby and the biggest secret of her life. Four days and five nights had seemed like an extremely long time.

But now that that week was coming to an end, it not only felt as if it had gone by fast, it felt as if it had gone by *too* fast.

And without fully accomplishing everything she'd hoped to, she thought as she stepped up to the full-length mirror to see how she looked.

Yes, she'd learned a little more about Ben, she reasoned as she turned to one side and then the other and ended up staring at herself straight on. But she hadn't learned enough. Instead, what little she'd come to know about him had only whetted her appetite to get to know him better. Certainly she hadn't gotten to know him well enough to jump into telling him she was pregnant.

But there she was, dressed in the jeans that were too tight for her to be able to wear for many more weeks and the sleeveless yellow polo shirt she'd just put on, and it didn't seem possible that this was her last night here. That tomorrow morning she would head back to Denver.

And that once she had, she would probably not be another thought in Ben Walker's mind....

She didn't like that idea at all.

But why *would* Ben think about her after this? Except maybe to have some passing memory of one night spent with his sister's friend at his class reunion.

Still, it didn't matter that there wasn't a reason for him to think of her. It only mattered that he wouldn't.

Unless she *did* tell him about the baby.

The moment that thought flashed through her mind she discarded it. She wasn't ready—she might not *ever* be ready—to do that. And she definitely wouldn't do it just to make sure Ben didn't forget her.

But she hated the idea that he might forget her so much that now that it had planted itself in her brain, she couldn't let go of it.

Just because of the baby, she told herself.

And because of the baby and the possibility that she might ultimately opt for telling Ben he was going to be a father, maybe she should do something to make herself memorable.

But what? she wondered as she tried tucking the polo shirt into her jeans. Then untucked it and tied it to one side. Then untied it.

Regardless of what she did with the polo shirt, though, she wasn't satisfied with the way it looked and so the first thing she decided was that the plain, almost-matronly shirt had to go.

Off it came and instead she took out a red T-shirt she'd thought she'd never have the courage to wear. It had an off-the-shoulder neckline, which meant that not only were her shoulders exposed, but that she also couldn't wear a bra.

But it was definitely memorable, she conceded as she returned to the mirror and held it in front of herself.

It was a shirt she'd bought to wear on the cruise she and Rob were supposed to take and never had. The baby-making cruise.

She removed her bra and slipped the T-shirt on, adjusting the folds that formed the straight line from just above her breasts to the middle of her upper arms.

Hmm. Now she remembered why she'd bought it—it was a knock-out shirt. A shirt she doubted anyone would ever forget her in.

Which made it a keeper.

Okay, a memorable shirt.

But that wasn't enough.

The second thing she did was not only refresh her mascara and blush, but also brush a light dusting of the blush across her bare shoulders. Then she added a little liner and a pale brown shadow to her eyelids, too, before applying two different kinds of lipstick to gain a darker color than she ordinarily wore.

Red off-the-shoulder shirt. More makeup. The whole effect made her look much sexier than usual but knowing that Cassie would be at dinner tonight, too, offered her a safety net that made that all right.

Plus, if she left Ben eating his heart out, that was something he would remember.

But as she took one last look at herself in the mirror and then turned away from it to put on her sandals it occurred to her that she wanted more than to just go back to Denver hoping Ben would think back on the way she looked tonight.

She wanted—she needed—more time with him. Time to sort out what she was going to do from here. Time to do what she'd begun on this trip. She still needed to get to know him so she could gauge how best to proceed with regard to the baby.

But what was she going to do? Suggest they become pen pals?

No, she had to work with the situation as it was, she decided. Which meant enlisting the only connections she had with Ben—or at least the only connections he knew about.

The school and Cassie.

Those were the connections he knew about.

So those were the connections she was going to have to play on, she realized, forming a plan.

She could announce tonight that she wanted to come back to Northbridge after the school was open to see it up and running. And that she wanted to visit Cassie.

To visit Cassie for a nice, *long* while since they'd had so little time together at the reunion and again this week.

Clair felt guilty for plotting to use her friend that way.

But it was a necessary evil. And she *would* spend time with Cassie, so it wouldn't be a complete fabrication.

But she would also spend time with Ben.

And why, she asked herself as she left the cottage and headed for the main house, did the prospect of seeing Ben again, of spending more time with him, make her feel so much better about leaving tomorrow?

Maybe that was something she shouldn't analyze, she thought.

She approached the rear of the main building then and could see Ben through the sliding glass door.

Dressed in a pair of jeans and a navy blue crewneck with the long sleeves pushed up to his elbows, he looked more amazing than any man had a right to look.

The way he looked was just…

Just the way it was. Pleasing to the eye but of absolutely no importance otherwise.

Although she *did* find her eye really, really pleased.

He spied her then, waved and called, "Hi. Come on in."

Clair crossed what remained of the patio to go through the sliding glass door into the kitchen, returning his hello when she got there.

Then she scanned the room for signs of Cassie, feeling all the more in need of a safety net suddenly.

"Cassie isn't back yet?" she asked, finding no one there but the jaw-droppingly handsome Ben.

"She's not coming," he informed her as he put a salad bowl in the refrigerator. "She just called. Mom threw her back out, and Reid gave her some pills for it that have made her dizzy—apparently you aren't the only one suffering with that lately. Anyway, Cass is going to sit with her tonight."

"Oh, dear. I hope your mom will be okay."

"She'll be fine. She does this periodically. We can't get her to retire from the dry cleaners and hoisting armfuls of clothes takes its toll on her now and then," he explained as he exchanged the salad bowl for another filled with tomatoes, onions and peppers and turned to the island counter.

That was when he actually took in the sight of Clair for the first time. And she could tell by his reaction that the red T-shirt had done the trick—he stopped short, his eyes widened and his eyebrows rose.

"Don't you look good," he said, sounding impressed.

Clair was torn between being uneasy at the loss of Cassie as her safety net tonight and being thrilled by his response.

"It's a celebration dinner," she reminded, explaining her appearance that way and putting some effort into downplaying it with her tone. "But maybe we should bring everything over to your mom's house—that way Cassie won't be left out and your mom will get dinner, too."

"Mom will be lounged out on the couch and won't want company, and I told Cassie I'd treat her to dinner later on to repay her for all her help around here. I wanted this dinner to be a thanks-for-your-help dinner for you, too, remember? And that would wreck it."

"I wouldn't mind."

"I would," he said pointedly, brooking no further discussion on the matter by pointing with his chin to one of the barstools on the other side of the island counter and changing the subject. "Sit while I chop all this stuff. I'll get you a glass of wine."

"No, no wine for me. It gives me a terrible headache and I'll have to leave before I get to eat," she lied in a hurry. "Besides, I'm not really thirsty. I'll wait for dinner and then just have some of that iced tea," she continued, nodding in the direction of the long kitchen table where two places were set across from each other at one end and a pitcher of tea waited.

Ben was too busy taking out a cutting board and a chef's knife to pursue it. Instead, while he went to work slicing and dicing the vegetables like a pro, he said, "Cassie wanted me to tell you that she'd come by first thing in the morning to say goodbye. But I'm hoping I might be able to fix it so that won't be necessary."

There was something leading in his voice and in the glance and mischievous smile he flashed up at her, and Clair bit. "How would you do that?" she asked, climbing onto the barstool.

"I just got to thinking today that this is Labor Day weekend and that I'll bet you aren't going back to work until at least Tuesday."

"Wednesday, actually," she informed him. "The day care is closed until then for the holiday."

"Even better. What I was thinking was that maybe I could talk you into staying. I have staff interviews scheduled from morning until night tomorrow and I'd like it if you could do them with me, give me your input. Then you'd also be around for Sunday and Monday's festivities, and you could leave on Tuesday."

Maybe the man was psychic. It was almost as if he'd known what she'd been thinking the whole time she was dressing.

Clair could hardly believe her luck. While she doubted that a couple more days here now would prevent the need to come back to Northbridge, a couple more days here now was still that much more time she could use. Plus, *he* was asking *her,* which meant no questions were raised yet about why she might suddenly be interested in coming back.

Not to mention that knowing tonight wouldn't be her last night here after all made her feel even better than plotting a return trip had.

Still, she didn't want to seem too eager.

So, over the sizzle of the sliced vegetables when he put them into a preheated wok, she said, "I don't know…"

"Do you have big plans for the holiday?"

"I wouldn't say they were *big* plans, no," she said, when the truth was she'd been invited, along with the rest of her staff, to a barbeque one of the preschool teachers was hosting.

"No hot dates?" he asked then, tossing another of those mischievous smiles over his shoulder.

"Definitely no hot dates," she answered with a laugh. "I don't have my sea legs for that yet."

"Then make some calls to cancel whatever not-big plans you had and stay," he urged as he judged the vegetables cooked, removed them and added strips of meat to the wok.

"What's going on for Labor Day?" she asked as if that were a factor when, in fact, she was thinking more about how terrific he looked from behind as he stood at the stove with his back to her. Those shoulders he kept glancing over were broad and straight. His torso was a muscular vee. And that derriere…

Lucky, lucky jeans to be riding *that* bit of male perfection.

But he was answering her question and she had to at least attempt to pay attention.

"You know Northbridge," he was saying. "We're doing it up right. Sunday is the last softball game of the season for the Bruisers—"

The Bruisers were the local team of men who played year-round sports, switching seasons from softball to football to basketball to keep in shape. And it was apparently working, if Ben's body was any indication.

"After the game," he continued, "there's the end-of-season blowout—that means dinner and a party at Adz. Ad is closing down for it but you know the whole town gets involved in just about everything so the place'll be packed. Then Monday there's the usual setup in the town square—contests and booths and the whole potluck supper. There's a band concert at night and the group marshmallow roast to wrap it up. And a good time will be had by all. You shouldn't miss it. Plus," he added, "I really would appreciate your expertise with the interviews tomorrow."

He tossed the vegetables back into the pan with the meat and then poured in a sauce, leaving Clair a few more minutes to pretend to be mulling his invitation to stay.

Then, as he scooped the meat and vegetables mixture onto a platter already lined with steamed rice, he said, "What do you say?"

"I'd say you're pretty amazing with that wok and the knife before it," she answered with a laugh, marveling suddenly at what he was doing.

But then she responded to his question. "Okay. I guess I can stay."

"Good choice," he said with a slow, sexy grin. "Then I'll definitely feed you."

"Was there a risk that you wouldn't?"

This time he arched only one eyebrow up at her. "If you'd have turned me down? Maybe," he countered.

He picked up the platter in one hand then, opening the refrigerator to retrieve the salad with the other and kicking the door shut once he had.

"Can I help?" Clair asked, realizing only in that instant that she should have offered some assistance earlier. Although Ben didn't seem to need it.

He pointed with his chin toward the table. "Ice for the tea, maybe. The bucket is in the freezer, already filled. If you bring that we can eat."

Clair got down from the barstool, did as he'd instructed and then followed him to the table where he was waiting for her to sit before he did.

"This all smells and looks wonderful," she said as she slid onto the benchlike seat. "I feel bad enjoying it without Cassie."

But not *too* bad.

"She'll get the leftovers and a dinner of her own later on," Ben assured, serving Clair first and then himself.

The food tasted even better than it looked and smelled, and Clair told him that, too.

Then, as they settled into eating, she said, "Give me all the grizzly details of the inspection."

"It wasn't too grizzly. Did you know Sam Schmidt? He's from around here, he was in Ad's grade in school."

"Vaguely," Clair said. "A tall, skinny guy with big teeth?"

"That's him. He did the inspection. He was thorough—I didn't get any breaks because he knew me—but he was friendly about it. That made it pretty painless."

Ben went on to tell her about the lengthy inspection as they ate. During the cleanup and afterward as they returned to sit at the kitchen table for more tea and the chocolate chip cookies Ben had baked for dessert, Clair gave him advice about the second inspection that would be done after the kids were in residence. She also regaled him with stories of inspection mishaps and impromptu social service visits that her father had endured, and he countered with his own experiences working at other facilities.

It was hardly a conversation that would have engrossed many other people, but besides the fact that they were both interested in the subject, just being with Ben and having his attention so intently focused on her made the time fly for Clair. Before she realized it, it was late.

"Is it nearly midnight?" she asked when she caught sight of the clock.

Ben glanced at it, too, clearly not having noticed the late hour, either. "Looks like it."

"And when is the first interview tomorrow morning?"

"Eight sharp."

"I'd better get out of here or we'll both be too bleary eyed to read résumés," Clair said, standing.

Ben didn't try to persuade her to stay, but he did seem reluctant as he pushed himself to his feet, too.

"I'll walk out with you—my legs can use a stretch," he said, following Clair through the sliding glass door.

There was the faintest breeze blowing—not enough to chill the warm night but just enough to bring with it the scent of fresh pine from the stand of trees in the distance.

For a moment Clair paused to breathe deeply. "Sometimes I forget how good Montana air smells," she said once she headed for the cottage again.

Something about that made Ben chuckle slightly. "It took me about two years being back here before I could appreciate it again."

"Why?" Clair asked, stepping up to the cottage door and opening it but remaining on the front stoop to go on enjoying the clear air.

"I spent so much time living outdoors when I was in Arizona that I was a lot more partial to the comforts of a roof over my head, indoor plumbing and a real bed complete with sheets and a pillow."

They were facing each other in the glow of the porch light again and the light from inside that she'd turned on, and she could see the wry smile that cocked one corner of his mouth upward.

"You lived outside in Arizona?" she asked, drinking in the sight of his handsome features as much as the scents she was breathing in—the faint, lingering scent of his aftershave mingling with that of the trees now that he was less than an arm's length away.

"Mmm. I spent a good portion of my time in Arizona outside, yes. The program was based on Outward Bounds programs. Only with more…let's say, muscle. The philosophy was that if we thought we were so tough, we could tough it out. That meant we had a bare minimum of supplies to live off the land."

"You roughed it outdoors for the whole three years you were there?"

"No, not for the whole time. But initially I did. Everyone did. Until we were judged more compliant and proved we were willing to follow instructions and obey the rules."

"Then you got to live indoors?"

"Then we moved up to the wards."

"Was that like a dormitory?"

"Dormitory sounds too nice. The wards were more

like barracks, I guess. One big open space without any amenities."

"What about a bathroom?" Clair asked.

"Outdoor facilities—johns in a separate building that was like a public park restroom. Showers were open-air."

Clair made a face. "It's a good thing you were in the desert if you always had to shower outside."

"Don't kid yourself, it can get cold in the desert, too."

"And once you'd made it to the wards? Was that as good as it got?"

"It was. And even after that, the slightest infraction sent you back to live outside again. Plus there were a certain number of mandatory days that had to be spent that way just to instill personal discipline."

"I guess that means you're an amazing camper," Clair said, trying to put a better spin on what sounded awful to her.

"I learned a lot of things at the ACA—how to cook your dinner tonight, for one."

"If you tell me there were grub worms in it because you learned how tasty they were when that was all you could forage for food in Arizona it will ruin my dining experience," she warned.

That made him laugh, a deep, barrel-chested sort of laugh that caused something inside her sparkle.

"No, no grub worms. But the Arizona Center for Adolescents was very big on turning us into self-sufficient, competent people. Part of their philosophy—the part I agree with—was that kids like me need to learn to put their energies into the productive projects rather than the unproductive ones. I learned a lot of skills there. Like carpentry—I worked my way through college doing construction."

Clair's eyes dropped to his shoulders and the hard muscles of his chest as it passed through her brain that working construction had probably honed his body to it's current art-form state.

Then she adjusted her line of vision back to his handsome face and found him smiling a small, secret smile that made her think he knew what had been going through her mind.

But still she tried to cover it up by saying, "Well, I appreciate the culinary lessons you learned there."

"Good," he said in a voice that had somehow gone lower and more sensual.

"So I guess I'll be over before eight tomorrow morning," she said then.

"Don't forget about breakfast. I don't want you getting dizzy on me again. Come somewhere between seven and seven-thirty, and I'll scramble eggs or make French toast or whatever strikes your fancy."

At that moment, staring up into his eyes once more, the only thing that struck her fancy was him. But she didn't say that.

Instead she said, "Okay. But no grub worms."

He smiled again, a lazy, sexy smile. "No grub worms. I promise," he said. Then he added, "I'm just glad you're staying."

She was, too. More glad than she should have been.

"It'll be fun. Well, interviewing potential staff won't be a laugh-riot, but the rest of the weekend should be fun. It's been a long time since I've had a Northbridge Labor Day."

"I'll make sure it lives up to your expectations," he said.

He reached only a single index finger to one of her bare shoulders, tracing it from an inch or so down her arm to where it curved into her neck.

"Did I tell you how terrific you look tonight?" he asked, leaving a trail of tingling sensations that rained all through her.

"I believe you did," she answered in a voice that was little more than a whisper.

"It bears saying again," he murmured.

His hand—big and warm and strong—came to rest along the side of her neck, and his thumb followed the edge of her jaw. Back and forth and back again....

It was soothing and exciting at once, and she couldn't help that her head tilted ever so slightly in that direction while still looking up into his eyes, basking in their warmth.

A voice in her head told her to say good-night and go in before he did more than caress her neck, her jaw-line. But she just couldn't pay attention to the voice. Not when this was so nice.

Then he began to close the distance between them. Leaning forward, downward. Slowly. Deliberately.

Clair's chin seemed to tilt upward just as slowly, just

as deliberately, and all on it's own even as that voice continued to warn her not to.

And then their lips met, and her eyes drifted closed, and her hand floated up to the solid wall of that chest that she'd glanced at moments ago.

Only tonight's kiss wasn't a quick one, the way both kisses of the previous evening's end had been. Tonight's kiss held, grew deeper, took a giant leap from those chaste, beginning kisses they'd shared the night before.

Tonight's kiss had lips that parted—his over hers and then hers in answer.

Tonight's kiss had tongues that played—his wickedly invading to chase hers, to dart and dash and blatantly dance with hers.

Ben's hand at her neck slipped around to cup the back of her head as that kiss deepened even more, and his other arm came around her, pulling her close. Close enough that she had to raise her hand to his shoulder and make way for her breasts to replace it against his chest.

That was when she became aware of how tight her nipples were. And how sensitive. So much more sensitive than they'd ever been before, and coming in contact with his body shot sudden, intense waves through her. Waves of pleasure. Waves of yearning for more. Yearning to feel his hands on them.

Their mouths were open-wide by then. Tongues were doing a far more serious dance. And with that sudden flash of yearning demanding its due, she knew she was very near the edge of no return. Near enough to finally heed that internal voice that was loud and insistent, warning her if she didn't stop this now, she never would.

Somewhere along the way her other hand had risen to his other shoulder and now she insinuated both hands between herself and Ben, pushing enough to remove her breasts from being tantalized any further by his chest.

For one brief moment she lingered long enough to absorb the feel of honed pectorals with her palms, but then she forced herself to push a bit more, to ease her mouth from his, to whisper, "Early morning tomorrow, remember?"

Not to mention that they'd agreed they would just be friends.

Ben went back to looking down into her eyes, to studying her face, to smiling the secret smile that had made her believe he could read her mind when she'd ogled him.

But he didn't persist.

Instead he agreed with her. "Right. Early morning," he repeated.

Then he took in a deep breath of the pine-scented air and let it out long and slow.

"Seven or so," he said, referring to the time they'd already discussed for breakfast, his voice husky and striking one more elusive memory of that night after the reunion. After making love…

"Seven or so," Clair said, taking her turn at repetition and trying hard not to think about that night spent in his arms. Being kissed by him. Touched by him. Made love to by him…

And it would have been so much easier if he would have let go of her. If he would have stepped back and given her some breathing room.

But he didn't. He leaned over once again and pressed warm lips to the outer-most tip of her shoulder, kissing the same path his index finger had taken and setting off a whole new wave of screaming demands in her body before he finally saved her from herself by finishing with one last kiss to the side of her neck before he did let her go, before he did step away from her.

And then, with another bit of cocky swagger in his tone, he said a simple, "'Night."

"Good night," Clair answered so feebly she sounded as if every ounce of strength had been sapped.

He turned and left anyway. And she went into the cottage and closed the door while she still could.

But once that door was closed she had to lean against it for a minute for support because he really had sapped every ounce of strength she possessed.

Or at least resisting him had.

Resisting him and resisting her own desires.

Her own surprisingly raging desires.

Desires that had sprung to life as if no time at all had passed since that night in June.

Chapter Six

Ben hadn't been exaggerating when he'd said Saturday would be a full day of interviews. Clair couldn't believe how many people they saw.

Had it not been for the occasional oddball—like the amateur opera singer who was convinced that forcing the boys to communicate only in song would solve all their problems, and demonstrating with a tune from *Tosca*—the day might have been unbearable.

Or if Clair hadn't been with Ben.

He managed to inject enough humor into the long hours to keep her going, to keep her amused and entertained—*Tosca* notwithstanding. Plus it was interesting to see him at work.

In spite of the fact that he'd said he wanted her input, he didn't actually need her there. He did ask her opinions and seemed to take them to heart, but he also had a clear vision of what he wanted in his staff members. Plus he was good at putting the candidates at ease, at drawing them out, at creating a friendly environment while still maintaining his authority and professionalism.

It was also clear that, for him, the kids put in his charge were to come first and that he expected that to be the case with everyone from the milieu counselors to the cooks. Anyone for whom that wasn't the case was immediately eliminated. As were those who were obviously inclined toward rigidity rather than evaluating the needs, the strengths and the weaknesses of each individual child and adjusting responses to them accordingly.

Once again Clair was impressed by the man who, despite the bad-boy remnants that still colored his edges, had evolved into an adult who knew his mind and was not timid about being a force to be reckoned with.

Although it wasn't lost on her that what served him—and what she had no doubt would serve the school—well, might translate into something more formidable when it came to her own situation with him.

The interviews had barely come to an end when Ben's cell phone rang that evening.

Clair continued organizing files while he took the call and when he hung up he explained what the concerned-sounding conversation had been about.

Lotty Walker's back had gotten worse, and Reid

wanted her brought in for an X-ray, and possibly sent to Billings for an MRI.

Clair went along, worried herself about the older woman who had provided her with a sense of home and family after her mother's death, and Saturday night became a family vigil at the hospital.

Not that Lotty was in any danger. It was just that the hospital was crowded, and back pain didn't have the priority that the car accident with five injured people did.

Even after Lotty's X-ray showed a probable herniated disk, the treatment she required to ease her misery was a time-consuming process. So, once everyone knew the older woman was not in any danger, the Walker children agreed that Cassie would take Ad's wife and Clair to their respective homes to get to bed before meeting her brothers at the Walker family home to help get Lotty situated for the night.

That left Clair being dropped off at the cottage by Cassie rather than walked home by Ben the way she'd been on evenings past.

Which was good, she told herself as she waved goodbye to her friend and went inside.

It was good that she and Ben didn't even have the chance to end tonight the way they had the night before. Good that they weren't even tempted to do again what they shouldn't have done at all.

And the fact that she didn't *feel* good about it? That she felt antsy and itchy? That even her long and tiring day and evening still somehow felt incomplete?

Better that than tempting fate, she decided.

But she found it impossible to fall asleep and instead lay awake in her bed, waiting for the sound of Ben's car. Wondering when she finally heard it if he might come to the cottage anyway—if only to say good-night.

Hoping he might…

He didn't though. And while she considered crossing the brick path to the main house to ask if he'd gotten his mother home all right, she fought hard to keep from doing that.

Of course he'd gotten Lotty home all right. And to go over and ask was really only an excuse to see Ben.

An excuse to see Ben without serving the purpose of getting to know him so she could make some decisions about the baby she was carrying, she admitted to herself.

But because that was the *only* reason she was supposed to spend time with him she refused to let herself budge out of bed.

Instead she stayed lying on her back, staring up at the ceiling, clutching the edges of the mattress in both fists as if to moor herself to that bed.

Fearing that it was going to be a long night.

A very long night of struggling with herself and that unruly attraction she had to Northbridge's bad boy.

The Walkers decided to make a brunch for their mother on Sunday, and since Clair was included, she offered to make cinnamon rolls as her contribution.

Apparently Cassie and Ben had a secret recipe for a

quiche that Lotty particularly liked, so Cassie stopped by the market on her way to the school for ingredients. Then she and Ben used the kitchen in the main house to produce two of their mystery quiches while Clair used the kitchen in the cottage to prepare her cinnamon rolls, merely visiting with them during the time she waited for her dough to rise and while the rolls baked.

When the food was ready, the three of them went to the Walker family home where they spent until late afternoon with Lotty, Luke, Reid, Ad and Kit.

By four o'clock Lotty assured them all that she would be fine on her own and sent them off to the Bruisers' last softball game of the season, scheduled to begin at five.

The team of local business and professional men had been instigated after Clair had left Northbridge. Her father had spoken of them and so had Cassie, but this was Clair's first experience attending a game.

It was held on the sports field that took up a portion of the grounds shared by the elementary, middle and high schools.

No professional event could have drawn more support—the bleachers were filled with townspeople and still there were more of them in chairs brought from home and on blankets on the ground.

"These guys just divide up and play each other?" Clair asked Cassie as the game got underway.

"Most of the time," Cassie confirmed. "They draw names out of a hat to make up two teams so who's on what side always varies and stays fair. The college still isn't big enough to have teams of its own, but sometimes enough of the college boys will get together to give the Bruisers a run for their money in one sport or another. But usually it's just these guys, yeah."

"Do all the games draw this kind of a crowd? At least half the town is here," Clair said, glancing at the other spectators from the blanket Cassie had supplied for the two of them.

"You know Northbridgers—it doesn't take much to bring them out or get them together. Besides, the guys put on a good game. It's fun," Cassie concluded.

And like everything that went on in Northbridge, a lot of spirit went into it. There was armchair-coaching, cheering, hooting and hollering and razzing from the stands—some of it answered good-naturedly by the players—and it made the game seem to belong as much to the onlookers as it did to the team.

Plus there was a fair share of milling around so folks could talk to each other, catch up and gossip.

Clair and Cassie were recipients of several of those visits to their blanket, but they both jumped when someone sneaked up from behind, plopped on the ground with them and said, "You two aren't fooling anybody— you're just out here for an eyeful of beefcake and buns."

Startled, Clair and Cassie simultaneously glanced over their shoulders.

But when Clair recognized their attacker, she said, "Lois!" and turned to give her old friend a hug.

"Lois Erickson, you nearly gave me a heart attack," Cassie chastised.

But the rebuke only made the other woman laugh. "I didn't get to go to the reunion and see Clair and I heard she was in town now, so when I spotted her I had to come over and shake things up."

"I'm glad you did. Well, I'm glad you came over, anyway," Clair said.

She meant it, too. She hadn't been as close to Lois as she had to Cassie through high school, but Clair had still considered Lois one of her best friends. After Clair had married and moved to Denver, Lois had gone to UCLA and remained living in California until only recently, so they hadn't seen each other in ten years.

"I was sorry to hear about your dad," Lois said then.

"I got your card and the flowers—they were both really nice," Clair told the dark-haired Lois who was as pretty as she'd ever been. Time hadn't dulled her beautiful skin or her dark eyes, and when she smiled it was just as bright and engaging as it had been when she was a teenager.

"Catch me up," Clair urged to get them back to more pleasant subjects as her old friend settled cross-legged on the blanket with them.

"Work, work, work," Lois obliged. "Until Friday I was a rep for a pharmaceutical corporation so I traveled until I was blue in the face and burned out. But beginning two weeks from now—after my vacation—I'll start with an Internet drug store that markets and sells over-the-counter meds, and I'll be able to work from home. Which is why I moved back to Northbridge. Although no one probably realizes I have because this is my first weekend home in sixteen days. Isn't it, Cassie?"

"Mmm. I guess so," Cassie muttered.

She didn't sound overly enthusiastic—either to see Lois or to confirm what Lois was saying. In fact, Clair had the impression that Cassie was slightly uncomfortable with Lois being there at all and wondered if Cassie was miffed with Lois for some reason.

If she was, Lois didn't seem to be aware of it. Or to notice that Cassie was suddenly utterly engrossed in the softball game and removed from what Lois was saying as Lois talked about the house she'd bought and was remodeling.

"And now that I'm living in town again," Lois concluded happily, "maybe Ben and I can be more than ships passing in the night. Who knows, we might even get somewhere."

Apparently Cassie had been paying more attention to the conversation than she'd seemed to be because she heard that and cast Clair a wary glance, as if to see her reaction to their friend's comment.

Clair's reaction was shock as she struggled to grasp what Lois had just said.

"You and Ben are...an item?" Clair asked feebly.

"We've had a few dates," Lois answered, her eyes finding him on the field and her pretty face easing into an expression that let Clair know that Lois had high—

very high—hopes for those few dates to blossom into much more.

"How…and when…did that happen?" Clair heard herself ask as her mind began to spin.

"It's strange, isn't it?" Lois responded, interpreting Clair's obvious surprise in her own way. "I mean, we've basically known each other our whole lives. But six weeks ago, when I was here for the closing on my house and for Gaby Marciano's and Bill Witcom's wedding—" Lois cut herself off to suddenly switch gears. "Gaby said you had RSVP'd that you were coming and I thought I'd get to see you. But then you weren't there."

"I couldn't come," Clair managed to mutter, recalling that that would have meant encountering Ben again just weeks after running out on him, so she'd rescinded her RSVP.

The brief response was enough of an answer for Lois, though, who went on with what she was saying.

"It was at the wedding reception that Ben and I just happened to sit at the same table. I had such a good time talking to him that I asked him to dinner the next week when I was back again."

Once more Lois's chatter took a detour. "I know, it was gutsy of me, but if there's one thing that working in sales has taught me, it's that. And am I glad…"

She paused again to locate Ben on the field and smile beatifically for a moment.

A smile that annoyed Clair something fierce.

But Lois didn't notice as she continued. "Since then

we've been out whenever I've come into Northbridge. But the problem—the problem I've had with all my relationships—is that I was gone too much to ever get into anything serious. But Ben and I just seem to be meshing so well. You know how it is when that happens. There are never any awkward silences, neither of us has to stretch for conversation, one date seems to pick up where the other one left off as if we haven't been apart at all, let alone for weeks while I've been gone. Anyway, now maybe something really can come of things between us. Wouldn't that be a kick? If Cassie and I ended up related?"

Clair couldn't bring herself to comment, and hoped her smile didn't look as pained as it felt, while all she could think was: *Am I supposed to be glad that the father of my baby is dating?*

But rationally she knew he was perfectly free to do that. That there was nothing to stop him. That there shouldn't be anything stopping him.

Of course he should date. He would probably eventually fall in love and get married—maybe to Lois. He would have kids. Kids other than Clair's baby.

Clair told herself that she should consider that a good thing. Support, in fact, if she decided not to tell him about the baby she was carrying. After all, he would have other kids. A wife. A family of his own. And she would likely only have this one baby. Given that scenario, not telling him about her baby had some justification.

Okay, not a lot of justification. But a little.

So she *should* be glad that the father of her baby was dating, but no matter how hard she tried, she just couldn't be.

Ben was *dating*.

It was as if someone had just forced her to think the unthinkable.

"Clair? Are you okay?"

Lois's voice penetrated her thoughts again and Clair realized she hadn't heard, or responded to, anything her friend had said in several minutes.

She yanked her attention back to what was going on around her and said in a hurry, "I'm fine."

"You looked like you zoned out on me."

"I was just thinking that it seems like things are falling into place for you," Clair said, only hoping that what Lois had gone on to talk about after Clair's mind had wandered fit that bill the way what she'd said before did.

It must have because again Lois interpreted Clair's reaction in her own way. This time it was as if Lois felt guilty for talking about how good things were in her life when Clair's wasn't so great.

"I had heard through an old buddy of Rob's that you and Rob got divorced," Lois said sympathetically. "I didn't know if I should bring it up, but I'm so sorry about that, too. I couldn't believe it. We all thought the two of you would be together forever. I just wish I could get my hands around Rob's throat and strangle him for what his friend said he did. Who knew he was such a rat?"

Clair laughed mirthlessly. "I had the same sentiments," she said. "But it's all water under the bridge now."

"I hope so. Are you seeing anyone?" Lois asked.

Clair assumed that Ben didn't count. Although it seemed strange to think that that was the case for someone with a presence as powerful as his. But she could hardly consider one night of getting carried away at a class reunion and now helping him to get his school going as dating him. Certainly not the way Lois was dating him. Or the way Lois meant.

So Clair said, "No, I'm not dating anyone."

"What about this array of guys paraded out here today?" Lois suggested, glancing at the field again. "You could just pick any one of them off the vine and count on getting a ruby-red beauty."

There was slightly more humor in Clair's laugh at that. And looking out over the Northbridge Bruisers at play she couldn't deny that Lois was right—there were more than a fair share of men who could turn heads.

Yet even as she surveyed the lot of them her gaze kept returning to one in particular.

The same one Lois had eyes for.

Ben.

Still she held fast to what she'd been convinced of before this trip. "I think I'm better off on my own."

"That's the hurt talking," Lois insisted. "You just have to get out there again—a little male attention is the best cure. It'll fix you right up. What about one of Cassie's other brothers? Look at them—Reid and

Luke are gorgeous, and they're good guys, aren't they, Cass?"

Cassie looked reluctant to be drawn into this. "I think I'm prejudiced," she said.

"Well, they are good guys," Lois insisted. "You could hook up with Reid or Luke the way I have with Ben and maybe we'd all end up related."

The way I have with Ben...

Lois's words rang in Clair's ears and stabbed at her like a million tiny needles.

"I think I'll just stick to being single for now," she reiterated.

"Isn't that your mom waving at you over there, Lo?" Cassie said then, pointing in the direction of the bleachers.

Lois reluctantly pulled her eyes off Ben to find the older woman who was, indeed, waving at them.

Lois waved back. "I'm staying with Mom and my aunt until my house is finished. I was hoping they'd sit through this to the end so I could talk to Ben after the game but it doesn't look like I'm going to get my wish."

Lois gave Clair another hug and then stood. "Cassie, will you tell Ben I'm home and I'll call him? I'm going to have to spend the holiday with Mom and Aunt Vanessa, but maybe he and I can have dinner Tuesday night. Tell him to hold it open for me."

"Say hello to your mom and your aunt," was Cassie's only response to that.

But Lois seemed to take that as Cassie's confirmation anyway because she once again switched her attention to Clair.

"Come home more often so we can see you," she ordered.

Clair merely smiled and nodded, making no commitment and fighting more of those sharp pins sticking her at the thought of coming to Northbridge to see Lois and Ben together.

"Happy Labor Day," Lois said then.

Clair and Cassie wished her the same and then watched her go off to join her mother before Cassie focused her attention fully on Clair again.

"Are you okay?" she asked.

"Am I okay? Sure, why wouldn't I be okay? It was good to see Lois," Clair said, hoping that saying it might make it true.

"You're pale as a ghost, and Ben told me you had some kind of dizzy spell the other day."

"That was nothing. I just hadn't had lunch. I don't know why I'd be pale now."

Cassie frowned and apparently saw through her attempt to seem undisturbed because she said, "I think Lois is taking things with Ben a little more seriously at this point than Ben is."

There were too many qualifiers in that sentence to make Clair feel much better. Cassie only *thought* Lois was taking things more seriously than Ben was, she certainly didn't seem sure of it. And only a *little* more seriously at that. *At this point*, could mean Lois was right in assuming there was hope for the future with Ben.

"It doesn't make any difference one way or another," Clair claimed.

Cassie ignored it. "I know what you told me on Friday, and I don't doubt that you're really, really gun-shy. But I think you're kidding yourself if you honestly believe something hasn't clicked for you with my brother."

"Cassie…" Clair said in a warning sing-song.

"I saw your face just now when you heard Ben's dated Lois. It was like she'd hit you alongside the head with a baseball bat. Nobody gets that way if they're as removed as you told me you are—or as removed as you may think you are."

"I was just surprised. I didn't know Lois and Ben had gotten together."

"Like I said, I don't think they've *gotten together* quite as much as Lois made it sound. They've been out a couple of times for dinner when she's been in town."

"And now she'll be in town all the time," Clair said, more to herself than to her friend.

"Yes, but I haven't heard Ben say anything like she just said—about hoping to see more of her or getting serious or she and I ending up related."

More of those needle stabs struck Clair and she couldn't help fidgeting. To pretend the source of her discomfort was something else she switched from sitting with her legs curled underneath her to sitting Indian fashion.

Then, trying hard to hide the feelings that had been brought to life by what she'd just learned, she said, "Ben could do worse than Lois."

"Yes, he could," Cassie agreed. "But that doesn't mean he wants her."

"Why wouldn't he? She's pretty and smart and fun to be with and…they're meshing—"

"But maybe he wants someone else."

"Like who?" Clair said, in a small voice, hating that she'd asked that question. Hating even more that she cared what the answer was. Hating more still that she was afraid Cassie was going to name someone who wasn't her.

But Cassie's only answer was an ambiguous, "You never know," before she went back to watching the soft-ball game.

Clair did the same thing, as if she honestly didn't have anything invested in this subject.

But no matter how hard she tried, she couldn't keep from watching Ben.

Anymore than she could keep from wondering if Cassie knew something she didn't know.

Something like who Ben *did* want.

And if it was her…

When the softball game was over all four Walker brothers headed to Ad's apartment to shower before the end-of-season party in Ad's restaurant below.

While they did that, Clair and Cassie went to see the

house Cassie had submitted an offer on that had just been accepted.

The house was a small two-bedroom bungalow only a block from the college campus.

Not only did Cassie want Clair to see it, Cassie also wanted to take some measurements of the empty rooms so she could begin to shop for furniture of her own.

Neither Clair nor Cassie had said any more about Ben or Lois or their relationship. But while Clair made all the right comments about her friend's just-purchased house, her mind was still stuck on the revelation, and on a new turn her thoughts had taken when she'd calculated how soon after her night with Ben at the reunion he'd begun to see Lois.

Rationally she knew Ben owed her no loyalty for that night. That there was absolutely no reason he couldn't have gone out with someone else the very next night if he'd wanted to. So there was also no reason for him not to have accepted Lois's dinner invitation weeks later.

What had she thought? Clair asked herself. That he'd been pining for her? That after their single night together, from which she'd fled the following day, he would go into some kind of extended mourning period during which he couldn't possibly even share a meal with another woman?

Of course she hadn't thought any of that.

It was just that she also hadn't considered that he might have begun a relationship with someone else between then and now.

And no amount of reminding herself yet again that it shouldn't matter to her helped.

She just kept imagining Ben and Lois together. And regardless of the fact that it *shouldn't* have mattered, it did.

Adz Restaurant and Bar was filling up fast when Clair and Cassie got there. By then Clair actually wanted to be anywhere else. Anywhere where she wouldn't have to see Ben at all. Where she wouldn't have to look at him and picture him in her mind's eye with Lois anymore than she already had.

But since she had to be there, she bought herself a few more minutes before she had to face Ben by telling Cassie that she was going to use the restroom.

It wasn't until Clair used the facilities, washed her hands and decided to freshen her lip gloss that she realized her purse was not slung over her shoulder the way she'd been thinking it was.

After a moment of panic and a quick search of the stall she'd just been in she recalled setting it on the floor next to the door of Cassie's house when they'd first gone in to look at it, and she knew she hadn't picked it up on the way out.

"Great. This night is just getting better and better," she muttered to herself.

She'd barely uttered the words when the bathroom door opened and Cassie joined her.

"Are you talking to yourself?" Cassie asked, since Clair was alone in the restroom.

Rather than answer the question her friend had asked, she said, "I left my purse at your house."

"Oh, I hate when I leave my purse somewhere," Cassie commiserated. "But at least you know where you left it. I'm sure I have anything you need for now. You and Ben can go by there on your way home after the party to get it. You saw where the key is—on top of the door frame."

Clair would have preferred to use the purse as an excuse to leave and not come back. To maybe claim she had a headache or something that would get her some time alone to sort through what she'd learned and her mixed-up feelings about it all.

But the transportation arrangements for the evening were that Cassie would meet up with her roommates at Adz and go home with them, and that Clair—who had driven herself, Cassie and Ben to the softball game— would drive herself and Ben home after the party so Ben was free to celebrate the end of the season by drinking with the rest of the team. That left her with no choice but to stick out the party and retrieve her purse later just the way Cassie had laid out for her.

"Here, take whatever you need," Cassie said, handing Clair her purse before heading for the stalls herself.

Clair set the purse on the counter that surrounded the sinks and took a look at herself in the mirror on the wall behind them to see what she really did need.

Her hair didn't require more than a finger-fluff and since she'd freshened her blush and mascara before leaving the Walker family home to go to the game, that was okay, too. Being able to reapply lip gloss would have been nice, but it wasn't necessary so she didn't search her friend's purse just for that.

"Thanks, but I guess I'm okay for now," she told Cassie when Cassie rejoined her.

"You look fine to me," Cassie assured her, glancing at her through the mirror as Cassie washed her hands. "Except that you're flashing again."

Clair knew what her friend was referring to and immediately glanced down at her top button. With the plain blue jeans she'd worn today she'd put on a white crocheted cardigan. It was lined in flesh-colored fabric so even though it gave the illusion of being see-through, it wasn't. Which allowed her to wear it alone and buttoned up the front. But for some reason the top button kept slipping from its hole. And since the V-neck was very deep—barely stopping where her cleavage began—when that first button came unmoored, it exposed a fair share of that cleavage as well as the swell of her newly larger breasts above the low-cut lace bra she had on underneath.

"You better keep an eye on me tonight and let me know when this does this," Clair told her friend as she refastened the button.

"You'll know whether I sound the alert or not. Every time you start getting more male attention than usual just figure that button has popped open again," Cassie joked.

"Great. Thanks," Clair countered sarcastically as they left the restroom.

The restaurant was even more packed by then, but Cassie led the way through the crowd to the table her brothers had in the corner. Seeing Ben again when they reached it caused Clair more of those needle-stabs that had begun during her conversation with Lois.

Needle-stabs that suddenly made her put a name to what she was feeling.

Betrayed.

That was what it was. She felt as if Ben had betrayed her by going out with Lois.

There was no justification for feeling that way and she knew it, but there it was and she couldn't help it.

Betrayed.

It was a feeling she was all too familiar with.

And she couldn't merely ignore it. Or go to him and act as if she wasn't feeling it. So she took the chair farthest away from him and told herself to just try to get through the evening, and that maybe, rather than staying through the Labor Day festivities the next day, she would depart for home in the morning.

Ben clearly found it strange that she kept some distance between them. He looked at her from beneath brows pulled together in a confused and curious frown.

But Clair pretended not to notice and instead instigated a conversation with Ad's wife, Kit, and her friend Kira.

Unfortunately acting as if she were engrossed in what they were saying wasn't the same as *being* engrossed in what they were saying and Clair was still intensely aware of Ben. Of the way he looked all freshly showered and shaved, dressed in jeans, too, and a plain white crewneck with long sleeves he'd pushed up to the middle of forearms that were tight and thick with muscles.

Sexy forearms that tapered to wrists and hands that were big and masculine and capable-looking.

Hands that might have touched Lois…

It was a thought Clair couldn't seem to shake all evening as she dodged and avoided as much contact with Ben as she possibly could.

Dodging and avoiding him was slightly easier—even though he tried numerous times to sit near her or talk to her—because there was such a big crowd jammed into the restaurant. But by the end of the evening when even the last of the celebrants were saying good-night, she had no choice but to join Ben in doing the same.

Still she couldn't keep a chill from her voice as they got into her car and she said, "I have to go by Cassie's new house because I left my purse there earlier."

"Okay," Ben said from the passenger seat.

He watched her fasten her seat belt but he didn't use his. Instead he angled himself so that he was nearly facing her, draping his arm around the back of her headrest.

"Want to tell me what's going on?" he asked then.

He didn't seem disturbed at all. But Clair knew he'd had a substantial amount to drink tonight and thought he might be too inebriated—or at least too relaxed—to be disturbed by anything.

Or maybe he was just asking what was going on at

that moment—as in where they were headed or what they were going to do now.

It was that interpretation of his question she chose to address. "I'm driving to the house your sister just bought," she reiterated coolly.

"That's not what I'm talking about. What's going on with you?"

Clair refused to take her eyes off the street she'd just turned onto to get to Cassie's house, despite the fact that his gaze was boring into her profile. "Nothing's going on with me," she said.

"Something is. You did your damnedest all night to steer clear of me."

"I thought that was best. Considering."

"Considering what?"

Clair pulled into what would be Cassie's driveway and turned off the engine. Then, still without so much as casting Ben a glance, she said, "Considering that you're involved with someone."

She got out of the car, slamming the door harder than she needed to. Harder than she'd intended to.

Ben got out, too, and followed her to the front door where she was straining to reach above the frame for the key.

For him all that was required was to raise his arm and that's what he did.

Then he held the key out to her. "I'm not *involved* with anybody," he said.

"Yes, you are."

He pulled his hand back just as she reached for the key, refusing to give it over after all. "I am not *involved* with anybody," he repeated more emphatically.

"I had a nice long talk with Lois Erickson at your game," Clair informed him, leveling a withering glare up at him.

He shook his head but it wasn't actually in denial. It might have been disgust—probably over being found out—but she couldn't be sure.

"Give me the key or unlock the door so I can get my purse," she commanded.

He shook his head again but he complied, using the key to unlock the door, then replacing it above the frame and opening the door for her.

Clair didn't hesitate to go inside, wanting only to get this entire day over with.

Ben followed her there, too, closing the door behind them and leaning his backside against it with his hands pinned behind him.

"I'm not involved with Lois," he said in a deeper voice that had lost all overtones of inebriation or joking.

"That's not what she says. She has big plans for your future together."

"After a couple of dates?"

"She said you'd had a *few* dates," Clair amended pointedly.

"Two or three? We're splitting hairs here. And either way, that doesn't make me *involved* with her. We had dinner a couple—maybe a *few*—times. That's it."

They hadn't gone farther than the living room of the empty house and it was lit only by the moonlight coming in through the oversize picture window. But even in the dim light it hurt Clair to look at him.

To avoid it she went to the archway that separated the living room from the kitchen and stood with her spine pressed to one side of it, facing the opposite side of it so she was once again in profile to him and had only to stare at the oak trim that bordered the connecting passage.

"Lois told me what a good time the two of you have had together. How much you're meshing…"

"We did have a good time," he admitted, surprising her.

"Then what are you doing going around kissing me?" Clair demanded before she had thought about saying the words out loud.

He didn't rush to answer that, leaving a silence in the vacant house that felt heavy to Clair, especially as she weighed all it might mean for him not to deny his relationship with Lois.

Clair's mind raced with possibilities and just when she mentally had Ben and Lois married with four kids, he said, "Not that I owe you an explanation, but I'll give you one anyway."

Clair raised her chin expectantly but still didn't look at him.

"Lois asked me to dinner after we talked a while at a wedding," he said. "And I accepted. She's easy to be with, and I like her just fine so we've had dinner again— maybe *twice*—since that first one. Are we *meshing?*

I'm not sure what that means, but we get along, we have some things in common, I'm not bored when I'm with her and she doesn't appear to be, either. Are we *involved?* There's no way I'd call it that—we've just had dinner. And after the way things ended up between you and me at the reunion I sure as hell didn't think I *couldn't* have dinner with her. Or with anyone else."

He'd managed to put the shoe on the other foot.

But Clair refused to take the defensive that easily. "I'm just saying that when you've started something with someone else you shouldn't be doing anything with me."

"I don't know that I've *started* anything with Lois."

"She thinks you have."

"Then she's jumping the gun."

"But you like her." That had come out as a strong accusation.

Yet again, Ben didn't deny it.

"She's a nice person and I went out with her because she had one important selling point."

"What's her *selling* point?"

"*She* hasn't been seriously involved with anyone in a long, long time."

Something about that also seemed like an offensive attack but Clair wasn't sure why. So she asked.

"That's an important selling point? That she hasn't been involved with anyone in a long time?"

"More important than you know," he said under his breath.

"Why?"

Once more he didn't answer readily, this time letting silence reign long enough to make her wonder if he was going to answer at all. Certainly giving the impression that he wasn't eager to tell her this.

But just when she began to think he wasn't going to, he said, "I was involved with Heather Crane—did you know her?"

The name was familiar to Clair but it took her a moment to place it. When she thought she had, she said, "A year ahead of us in school, cheerleader?"

"Her father sold used cars. Her mother had that shop that only sold frog-themed things for a while," Ben said, expanding on the details as confirmation.

"Right. I didn't know her as a friend but I vaguely remember who she is."

"Well, I was involved with her," he repeated. "About two years ago."

"*Seriously* involved," Clair guessed from his ominous tone.

"Serious enough to want to marry her," Ben said, his voice echoing with even more ominous undertones.

"But she didn't want to marry you?" Another guess.

"I was her first relationship after a messy divorce. *Right* after her divorce—she came into Adz to drown her sorrows after leaving court to get the final divorce decree. I was working the bar for Ad because his regular bartender was out sick. We ended up spending the weekend together— not in bed, but together almost the whole weekend."

"She went from divorce court to spending the weekend with you?" Clair summarized, amazed when she thought about the day her divorce had been finalized. "I can't imagine that."

"It wasn't smart. On either of our parts," he agreed.

"And that was the start of it?"

"That was the start of it. We saw each other for the next eight months—exclusively. We got closer and closer. I fell for her."

His voice was deep and quiet and Clair could tell he wasn't opening up about this easily.

Still, though, he continued. "But when I let her know that I was looking toward a future with her I got my eyes opened," he said with a chuckle that was void of humor. "She said that the time we'd been together had really been a period of getting her sea legs. That after just ending a marriage she was nowhere near ready to settle down again. That, in fact, since I'd helped her get over the hump of the hurt, it was time for her to move on— to move out of Northbridge and start over. By herself."

"Ouch," Clair said softly.

"Yeah, well..." Ben said with another mirthless laugh. "I learned then and there that the rebound guy isn't the guy who ends up getting the girl. The rebound guy is the guy who rebuilds the girl's ego and self-esteem. Who makes her feel attractive again. Who gives her the courage and the confidence to get back in the game."

"And who gets hurt himself," Clair said just as softly.

He didn't respond to that and in the silence that was

left this time she wondered if any of her attraction to him was due to the fact that she could probably be considered on the rebound herself.

But when she turned her head to look at him and took in the sight of that big buff body, of that hands-down handsome face, she knew there were a whole slew of other reasons to be attracted to him, on the rebound or not on the rebound.

"So, this thing with Lois," she said, her voice no longer hostile the way it had been since leaving Adz. "It didn't come about because you've had some deep-rooted crush on her since you were in diapers?"

That made him smile and lightened the tension. "Hardly," he said, pushing off the door and slowly crossing to her, stopping under the archway, too, to face her.

"And how far has this noninvolvement gone?"

"As far as Billings a couple of Saturdays ago because she knew a good place to get seafood in the city."

There was a note of teasing in his voice now so Clair didn't know if he was purposely misunderstanding her question or if her question had been too ambiguous.

But what she was wondering about was important to her so she tried again. "You've had three dates."

"Okay."

"I've heard that the third date can be…the big one."

"One's been pretty much like another," he said, still not revealing much.

"Have you kissed her?" Clair persisted.

He stepped closer, standing near enough that she could smell the lingering scent of his cologne and feel the heat, the power, emanating from his big body. Near enough that she had to tilt her head far back to look up into his face. Into the crooked, devilish smile he was aiming down at her.

"I have kissed her," he admitted in a confidential voice.

He raised one hand and, with his thumb, rubbed a tiny spot on her cheek. "Once here." Then he moved his thumb to her upper lip, smoothing it with a feather-stroke. "And once here."

He leaned forward so that he was almost nose-to-nose with her.

"But as kisses go, they weren't much more than friendly little pecks." His thumb slid down to her chin where his other fingers formed a shelf underneath it to tilt her head back a bit more.

"And I can promise you," he said in a lazy drawl, "that I've never kissed her like this."

His mouth came over Clair's then, claiming it with lips parted, warm and adept, with a familiarity that somehow made them seem to belong to her and her alone.

And heaven help her, she kissed him back. She told herself not to. She told herself that this wasn't what she'd come to Northbridge for. She told herself that this was what had gotten her into her current predicament in the first place. She told herself that he was seeing Lois, that Lois had high hopes.

But none of it made any difference. For that moment

he was hers. He was kissing her in a way he'd never kissed her friend.

So, so good…

And then she stopped telling herself anything at all and merely let that kiss be her world.

That kiss where he parted his lips even more and she did, too.

That kiss where his tongue darted in to find hers, to claim that as confidently as he'd claimed her mouth at the start. To circle and soothe. To excite and exalt in. To tease and torment without conscience.

Somehow along the way his hands had found the sides of her face, holding her to that kiss, taking charge and caressing at once.

And hers had gone to his chest. To honed pectorals that were like mounds of granite.

Kissing him, touching him, having him touch her, awakened her every sense and raised more needs within her. Needs that brought her nerve endings to the surface of her skin. Needs that made her hate that there were even inches separating their bodies when what she wanted was to be so tightly against him that there would almost be no room to breathe. Needs that hardened her nipples and made her breasts long for his attention. Long for those strong hands. Those nimble fingers. Those lips and teeth and that tongue.

She didn't intend to arch her back away from the wall's edge. To thrust those yearning breasts toward him. It just happened. And when it did, she tried to make it into something that didn't seem so demanding of his notice by raising her hands to his shoulders, to the thick column of his neck and around to his nape where she could toy with the bristly hair there.

But he wasn't fooled. Or maybe he was just thinking the same thing she was. Because his right hand began a slow descent then, trailing the backs of his fingers down the hollow of her throat, along the scalloped edge of her sweater's low V-neck, to one breast.

Only he didn't enclose that breast in his hand as she anticipated that he would. Instead, in no hurry at all, he taunted her by still only using the backs of his fingers to scarcely—oh-so-scarcely—brush across the very tip of her nipple.

Whether it was her own supersensitivity or the allure of that almost nonexistent touch, less was more. Less was enough to make that nipple kernel into a tight knot and strain through the confines of the lacy bra she wore. Less was enough to arch her back another degree, enough to elicit a soft groan from her throat and make him smile even as his mouth opened wider still over hers and his tongue grew even more bold and brash.

Then, just when she wanted his whole hand on her so badly she thought she might press it to her herself, he let his palm encase her nipple and formed his fingers around that full, firm globe.

Her memories of that night they'd spent in her room after leaving the reunion were vague and blurry, yet she was convinced that nothing that had happened then felt quite the way his hand on her breast at that moment felt. Nothing had ever felt that remarkable and she couldn't stop a second, more primitive groan from rolling from her throat. She couldn't stop herself from moving farther away from that wall and into his grasp. She couldn't stop herself from curling one of her legs around one of his and bringing the lengths of at least that part of their bodies together.

Bodies she wished were free of every stitch of clothes so that not only would her breast be bared to his caress, but so would the rest of her. So that he would be bare to her.

With that in mind, she pulled his T-shirt from the waistband of his jeans and wasted no time plunging underneath, allowing her hands, at least, to travel the silk-over-steel feel of his broad back, slightly digging her fingers into his flesh, massaging, kneading, learning the swell of each muscle.

Mouths opened as wide as they possibly could and he thrust his tongue in and out in rapid succession before he tore away from her to kiss, to nibble, to nip a path that followed the one his hand had blazed.

Only this time when he reached the lowest portion of that vee there was no teasing, no tormenting. His hand abandoned her breast long enough to pull her sweater down, to push her breast up and out of her bra so that his mouth could capture it with a fiercer intensity than any of his plundering kisses.

An intensity answered in the sensations that washed

through her, that dropped her head back against the wall, that opened her mouth and made her breath a sigh that was pure, raw pleasure as her fingertips delved even deeper into his back.

And then he stopped.

At first she thought it was so that they could move out of that archway, so that they could shed clothes and lie on the floor and do all her body was crying out to do.

But instead Ben laid his forehead to her collarbone for a moment and then straightened up. He drew his head back, clasped the wall above her with both hands and breathed in bottomless breaths as if using the air to gain some control.

"I just finished telling you I know better than to be the rebound guy and here I am…" he said in a raspy voice.

Oh, that…

So, he did think she was on the rebound. And she wasn't sure that she wasn't and couldn't convince him otherwise.

Besides, now that she was catching her breath, too, sanity had reasserted itself, and she remembered her own reasons why it was better not to go on with this.

She adjusted her clothes and ducked out from under his arms. "I'll get my purse," she said.

He didn't say anything and he didn't budge, he just went on standing there, doing a sort-of push-up against the side of that archway. But what little light came in through the kitchen window left him in silhouette and one glance at him in profile—full-body profile—left no doubt that he'd been as aroused as she had.

So Clair allowed him his moment. She turned and crossed the empty living room, retrieving her forgotten purse and going out to her car to wait for him.

When he joined her there he didn't say anything and neither did she, leaving them in silence on the entire drive back to the school.

When they arrived, Clair parked her car near the cottage and, still without talking, they got out.

But Ben didn't leave her to go to her door alone. He walked her there, waiting until she'd unlocked and opened the cottage door to reach a hand to the side of her neck to keep her from going in, urging her to face him.

"You do things to me," he told her then, his voice still deep and quiet, for her ears only. "The kind of things that make me act without thinking. That's how I used to get in trouble."

Something about that made him grin and in that instant Clair knew she was seeing the wild streak in him. The wild streak that had reveled in the joyrides and pranks before they'd gone bad.

And it was dangerously appealing.

"But you try to avoid trouble now," she reminded him.

"Yeah," he said as if there might be a part of him that regretted that.

But beyond looking down at her with those penetrating eyes, beyond studying her face as if he were committing it to memory, beyond giving her the impression that with a little less self-control he'd be sweeping her off her feet and into her bedroom, he didn't do anything.

He just stayed there a moment before his hand at her neck caressed her much as he'd caressed her breast earlier. Then he pulled away.

"I'll see you tomorrow," he said, turning on his heels to go.

"Tomorrow," Clair repeated, remembering only then that she'd been planning to cut the extension on this trip short and leave the next day.

But as she stepped inside the cottage and closed the door she didn't even entertain that possibility anymore.

Instead she just stood there in the dark, closing her eyes and thinking about what had just happened at Cassie's house.

And how good it had all felt.

And how much she wished it had gone all the way…just one more time.

Chapter Seven

Northbridge loved its holiday and seasonal festivals, carnivals and celebrations. All the tall wrought-iron streetlamps along Main Street and surrounding the town square were wrapped in red and purple crepe-paper streamers, and the flower boxes that surrounded each one were planted with red and purple pansies.

A huge banner announcing the Labor Day festivities was stretched across the end of the intersection where Main Street formed a *T* with the east-west running South Street—named because it was the southern-most border of Northbridge proper.

On the other side of the intersection was the town square, an acre-wide expanse of lawn peppered with oak trees. The centerpiece of the square was an octagonal-shaped gazebo. Five steps led from the ground up the redbrick base to the platform where a whitewashed cross-buck railing bordered the sides, and whitewashed round pillars braced the sharply pointed, bright red roof that was topped at its point with an octagonal cupola.

Around the gazebo there were stands and booths set up to sell fresh produce and any number of other home-made foodstuffs and crafts the locals had tried their hand at producing. There were also a number of tents erected to keep the elements from dampening the various contests that were held—the pie-baking contest and its cousin the pie-eating competition, the quilt contest and subsequent auction, the hoola-hoop contest and a number of other events for the children.

There were two other, larger tents, as well. One under which a stage had been built for band and choir performances and the awarding of all prizes, and another food tent that contained an L-shaped buffet table where the pancake breakfast, the hot dogs and hamburgers luncheon and the potluck supper were set out, served and then eaten at the long cafeteria tables that had been brought over from the school.

It had been a long time since Clair had attended one of these functions and being there brought back many fond memories. The entire town got in the spirit, competing in the contests or cheering on the competitors, sampling and eating an abundance of food, playing the games, donating to the causes that had set up booths and stands for that purpose, and just all-round enjoying themselves.

There was only one thing Clair could find fault with throughout the day and evening, and that was that she wasn't alone with Ben. They were with his family, plus there were the rest of the townsfolk Ben and Clair hadn't already seen or spoken to at any other recent events who wanted to chat or gossip or catch up or offer best wishes to Ben for the opening of his school.

Clair told herself it was probably for the best that she wasn't alone with Ben, that she hadn't even been alone with him from the get-go that morning. Not being alone with Ben had spared Clair discussing what had happened—and nearly happened—the previous evening. All those chaperones also kept at bay any temptation to repeat, or finish, what had ended the night before.

But still, when Clair had showered and washed her hair and put on the filmy flowered halter sundress in preparation for this day, she'd imagined herself and Ben together through the Labor Day festivities. She hadn't imagined that they would just be part of a big group in which she spent more time with Cassie, and Ben spent more time with his brothers.

And the fact that it was Clair's last day there, her last day with Ben, seemed to be an underlying thought through it all.

It did pass through her mind that she'd thought the same things, felt the same things, two days earlier. And that here she was, having had those two more days with him, again thinking and feeling that she hadn't had enough time with him.

But she tried not to dwell too much on why that was. Instead, she once more accepted that she wasn't ready to make any decisions yet about whether or not to tell him about the baby and opted for continuing to postpone that, at least, until she returned to Denver.

Denver, where she'd be away from Ben. On her own turf. Where she'd be sure of thinking straight. Straight and uninfluenced by anything but the facts and her own feelings.

Uninfluenced by the way Ben looked, which was a sight to behold in a pair of aged jeans that fit him like an old friend and a dark blue dress shirt he wore with the sleeves rolled to his elbows.

Uninfluenced by the sound of that deep voice that seemed to roll over her like warm, honeyed whiskey. Uninfluenced by the sea breeze scent of him or the smoky intrigue of those blue-green eyes, or that slight cleft in the center of his chin. By the whole attitude that was Ben—confident, brash, bold, just a little deliciously devilish under the surface of it all. And sexy.

Sexy, sexy, sexy…

Yes, it was definitely better not to have that influence.

When the potluck supper was finished there was a band concert to complete the day's entertainments. That lasted until long after dark before ending so the crowd could filter out of the square and go home to face their workweek.

Clair said her goodbyes to the Walkers and only a good-night to Cassie who was slated to have breakfast with her before she left the next morning. Then Clair and Ben found Ben's SUV where it was parked across the street in the church lot.

"Did you have a good time?" he asked as he opened the passenger door for her and she got in.

"I did," Clair said, omitting the fact that she might have enjoyed herself a little more had she had a little more time with him.

Ben closed the door and went around to the driver's side to get in. "I don't think you've missed seeing anybody this trip, have you? It seemed like everyone you might not have run into during the week tracked you down today," he said as he started the engine.

"It certainly seems like I've talked to the whole town along the way," she confirmed with a laugh. Then, watching for his response out of the corner of her eye, she added, "No Lois today, though. I thought for sure she'd be there." And she'd dreaded the idea of seeing Lois seek Ben out, of maybe even hearing them make arrangements to see each other again after she was gone.

"No, no Lois today," Ben said. "So let's not take her home with us, either."

Clair was willing to accept that suggestion because she didn't want the other woman invading this time she finally had alone with him. "Okay," she agreed.

It was Ben's turn to glance at her. "It occurred to me

last night, though—after talking about Lois and Heather—that you owe me one. At least one."

"One what?" Clair asked, confused.

"One look into your relationship history."

Clair made a face. "You definitely don't want to take *that* home with us," she said.

"Then we won't go home," he countered, bypassing the driveway he should have turned onto to get them up to the school and heading farther out into the open countryside beyond it.

"Oh, not fair play!" she accused.

He flashed her that bad-boy half grin and went on driving, turning at the next fork in the road.

"Have you seen the work that's been started on the old bridge?" he asked then.

"No, I've heard a lot of talk about it, though."

"Then I think that should be the place."

"I'd like to see the work on the bridge anyway," she said, letting him know that wherever they ended up, telling him about her failed relationship and marriage was not a foregone conclusion.

But Ben just cast her another of those half grins and followed the narrow road that was little more than a buggy path through a densely wooded area.

The bridge didn't come into sight until they reached a clearing. It spanned what had once been a river to the west of town. The river was little more than a stream now and a concrete bridge carried traffic over it as a portion of South Street that led out into the countryside west of town. The old road and bridge were just relics of days gone by now.

But since the covered bridge was the town's namesake, the town counsel had voted to preserve it.

"I never understood why the bridge was considered the *north* bridge—and inspired the town's name as Northbridge—when it's actually southwest of town," Clair said. "Do you know?"

"I do as a matter of fact," he said as he pulled off the road just a few yards from the bridge and parked.

"Fill me in."

"Okay, here's the history lesson of the night. At first there wasn't any town at all, just a few farms and the bridge across the river to get to them from the main road from Billings. The bridge was north of the farms, so it was referred to as the north bridge. When the town proper cropped up it needed not to interfere with the farmland, so it went north of the bridge. But then the bridge linked the town and the farms so it was important enough to be the namesake and since the bridge had always been called the north bridge…"

"Ah, I get it," Clair said.

The moon was nearly full and when Ben turned off the headlights it provided enough illumination to see the wooden bridge.

Crosshatch bars ran the length of both solid sides as well as the railing that supported posts holding a shingled roof.

Ben pointed a long index finger in that direction.

"You can see where they've started to replace the old weathered wood with new. It'll basically be completely rebuilt by the time the project is complete, and then it'll be painted red—apparently that's what it was originally."

"And it'll look like something you'd be more likely to see back East," Clair supplied.

"I think that's the goal," Ben confirmed. "Come on, I'll show you what I did when I was in big trouble at home and maybe we'll do some stargazing," he added then.

He reached into the back seat for the blanket they'd brought in case all the chairs for the concert had been taken and they'd needed to sit on the grass. Taking it with him, he got out of the car and came around to Clair's side.

She didn't wait for him to open her door and was outside to meet him when he got there.

"You did something out here when you were in trouble at home?"

"When the heat was on," he said ominously.

But he didn't explain. He merely took her hand and led her to the bridge.

The act of taking her hand like that caused Clair's mind to go blank and all her focus to be on the fact that he'd actually done that. As if it were something he'd done a thousand times before. As if he had the right.

Of course she didn't pull away from his grip to let him know he *didn't* have the right. She allowed her own fingers to curl around that hand while the heat of it enveloped her and permeated her skin in a way she liked. A lot…

He led her across the bridge—stopping inside to

point out the work that was being done on the roof—and then headed out the other side.

"They're turning this area into a park, you know," Ben informed her then.

But Clair was more conscious of him releasing her hand once they left the bridge and went onto the bank of the stream where he needed the use of both his hands to spread the blanket on the small grassy knoll beside the lazily flowing water. She didn't care much about anything but the loss of that hand around hers.

When he had the blanket spread out he took off his shoes and socks and laid down on it. Braced on his elbows, he used one hand to pat the area beside him. "Might as well be comfortable to stargaze."

Clair spent a moment staring down at him, at that blanket, thinking about whether or not to join him. And how dangerous she knew it was if she did. Because there he was, looking so good, and she really, really wanted to be there with him.

But what if she did join him and things got out of control again, the way they had at the reunion, the way they had last night?

It seemed possible when they'd be lying on a blanket together, under the stars.

But it was her last night there, she reminded herself. And she was finally getting some time alone with him. What was she going to do? Demand that he take her home and deny herself this small thing that she'd been wishing for the entire day?

Maybe nothing would happen, she reasoned. It had been Ben who had stopped things the previous night, after all. Maybe he genuinely only wanted to look at the stars, talk, learn about that relationship that he didn't want to be the rebound guy for.

And if not? If things started up between them again?

Just thinking that set off little butterflies in the pit of her stomach. Little flutters she couldn't stop. Little flutters of possibilities she knew she shouldn't encourage.

But all she could think was that this *was* her last night.

And before she considered anything else, she kicked off her shoes, too, and sat on the blanket with him.

"So, when the heat was on at home, this is where you came?" she asked, positioning herself so she was facing him and curling her legs to one side.

Ben looked up at the sky. "I'd grab a blanket, sneak out my bedroom window and spend the night out here, hoping things would cool down before I went back. It was the perfect place—the bridge hasn't been used in decades, and, even though the mayor thinks refurbishing it and sprucing up things around it will induce folks to come out here, it isn't a big draw. Plus, when the weather was nice I could sleep on the ground under the stars, and when it wasn't so nice I'd set up in the bridge for shelter."

"Did your family know you came here?"

"Not at first. The first time I did it my mom thought I'd run away and reported me to the cops. They found me out here, rousted me and dragged me home. I was in more trouble then. But somewhere during the ensuing screaming match I said I'd just been getting some air to cool off, taking a time-out. After that, when I left, she didn't send anybody after me. I only did it when my temper and hers were both flaring—I think she saw the wisdom in the cooling-off period and just accepted it."

"So you had some preparation for the outdoor portion of the Arizona placement."

"That's what my mother thought when she was making her decision about where to send me. She figured that the wilderness training was right up my alley because I'd spent so many nights sleeping out here. Little did she know just how different the two actually were," he added wryly. "It's a lot different to leave home with a full stomach, sleep outside and go back home in the morning in time for breakfast, than to be set down in the middle of nowhere with nothing but a few staples, knowing you have to fend for yourself for days and days on end."

"Did you tell her that?"

"So she'd feel guilty? I'd given her enough grief. She thought she was doing what was best, and easiest for me."

Ben went from looking at the sky to pointedly looking at Clair, his expression letting her know he wasn't giving any ground. "And here we are again. I've told you all about my rotten youth and all the details of the hell I put my family through, along with telling you about my love life, but you're still playing mystery woman with me."

"Mystery woman?" she repeated with a laugh. "I'm hardly that."

"Great, then you'll give me the lowdown on *your* love life."

"There's just a single note—a sour one. I don't know that that counts as a whole *lowdown*."

"A single note?"

"There's only been one guy."

"Rob Cabot—ex-husband and scourge of the reunion," he said.

"Right."

"Not an amicable divorce," Ben guessed, apparently from her tone of voice.

But Clair still wasn't sure she wanted to get into it.

Ben saw her reluctance and said, "Come on. I told you mine, you tell me yours. Start with the way you met and ease up to the rough stuff. Did your eyes first lock over spaghetti in the cafeteria or after he'd made the winning touchdown at the homecoming game or what?"

"Apparently you flooded out the homecoming game," she reminded, joking to stall for time.

"That would have been the year *before* you came here and had the chance to meet the golden boy."

"That's what he was, too—the golden boy. Class president, quarterback, star of track and field, the boy-most-likely-to-succeed," Clair confirmed because she recalled that Ben had said he didn't remember much about Rob from school.

"So he was a catch."

"That's what everyone thought," Clair confirmed.

But she still didn't rush to talk about her past and Ben switched positions, rolling to lie on his side, propping his head on one hand and using the other to take one of hers again, lending that strength and heat for support, rubbing the back of her hand with his thumb to soothe her nerves.

"Come on," he repeated in a voice that beckoned her irresistibly.

"I thought it was poor form to talk about my divorce to other men."

"Not if they ask," Ben instructed.

After another minor hesitation Clair decided it wasn't the secret of the century and conceded. "Okay, okay, okay."

"You met over a Bunsen burner…" Ben said as if to get her started.

"No, just at school. Nothing monumental. I was the new girl, he was the big man on campus for our grade and we liked each other."

"And was it serious from day one?"

Clair laughed slightly. "You know how kids are—*everything* is serious. But I moved here when I was fourteen. Rob was fifteen even though we were in the same grade because his birthday fell a few days later than the cutoff for starting kindergarten. But to say we were *serious* from day one? We weren't engaged by Christmas of ninth grade, if that's what you mean."

"How long did it take to get to that point?"

"Rob asked me to the first dance of freshman year, and we were together from then on."

"There weren't even any dramatic breakups and getting-back-togethers?"

"The only breakup was the divorce and there won't be any getting-back-togethers, no," she said wryly.

"And the engagement?"

"Senior year. He gave me a ring for my birthday in March."

That made Ben flinch. "You were still babies."

"We were very young," she agreed. "He had turned eighteen a few days after senior year started, I turned eighteen in March. We were married a week after graduation."

"Babies!" Ben shouted for effect.

"It isn't what I'd want any child of mine to do."

"Okay, you were barely out of high school and married," he summarized to keep the story going.

"Our parents continued helping us financially so we could both go to college—which we did—"

"And things were good through that?"

"We were still madly in love," she confirmed. "We graduated, I started work at the day care I run now, he got hired on at a bank, on the executive track, and things went on being good. We both moved up the ladder at work. We saved for our dream house and got that. And then it felt like it was time to start a family."

"It felt like that to you? To him? To you both?"

"To me, mainly. But he got on board—"

"No pun intended," Ben said with another of those wicked smiles.

"No pun intended," she confirmed, not taking offense because his humor helped keep the much-less-than-amusing feelings she had at bay.

"So, baby-making. I know you don't have any kids," Ben said to encourage her to continue.

"We started trying about three...no, three and a half years ago. And nothing happened."

"You mean, no sex or just no baby."

The evil-around-the-edges smile let her know he was still easing the tension with humor.

"No baby," she answered. "For the first year we just kept trying, but after that I went to see a doctor. He tested us both, found nothing wrong with either of us that should have caused us to be infertile, and sent us home to keep on trying."

"That doesn't seem so bad. Why do you make it sound like it was?"

"The whole trying and failing, trying and failing took a toll."

"On you? On him? On the marriage and relationship?"

"Yes," she said, the simple word encompassing it all. "I was frustrated. And, I admit, obsessive. I just wanted a baby so bad—" Her voice cracked with only the memory of how badly she'd wanted a baby, of how awful it had felt not to have that happen month after month, to begin to fear that it never would.

Ben squeezed her hand and it helped her go on.

"And Rob..." Clair shook her head. "Rob was a person who had succeeded at everything. Who had never been denied anything, really, and who couldn't stand to be. He was definitely the golden boy and he'd never been anything less. But there we were, doing everything imaginable to have a baby and it wasn't working. For the first time in his life his game plan wasn't panning out. He was *failing*—"

"That word seems to be a key here."

"It was a big deal to me that we might not have a baby, but to Rob it became an embarrassment. Rob Cabot didn't *fail*. That wasn't something he could accept. Certainly not in himself or in anything he did. And so two things happened…"

Clair took a deep breath to give herself the courage to say what those two things were.

"First of all he decided that there had to be a problem that the doctors and all the tests had just missed. And that the problem had to be mine. That there was something wrong with me."

Ben's sigh sounded on the verge of anger and he shook his head. "Of course," he said. "If there was something wrong it couldn't have been the golden boy."

"Not in Rob's world," she confirmed.

"And what was the other thing that happened," Ben asked as if the first was too absurd to merit more attention.

"The second thing that happened was that I guess Rob needed…" Clair shrugged. "I don't know, his ego boosted or to prove his manhood or something that takes a cliché to explain. But he had an affair."

When she said that her voice had been so quiet it was almost inaudible and again Ben squeezed her hand.

"Actually," she said to qualify that last statement, "that makes it sound like some passing indiscretion or something."

"But it was more than that."

"A lot more. It was as if, I don't know, as if he had something to prove. Which I think meant that he wanted to flaunt it. But I was so focused on the baby issue that I was missing it—his withdrawal, working late and on weekends suddenly, a lot of business trips when he'd never had to make business trips before, secret phone calls he'd end abruptly when I came into a room— things that should have made me suspicious except that I was only thinking *baby, baby, baby.*"

"So he finally told you?"

Clair shook her head sadly. "I came home from work about a month after my dad died and found Rob in our bed with the woman."

Ben grimaced at that and shook his head. "Oh, brother. Could he have sunk any lower?"

"As a matter of fact he could," she said. But she saved that part of the story and continued with the portion she was already addressing. "I think he wanted me to literally see it for myself. To see what a stud he was. Anyway, I left and that was it. We filed for divorce and the day after it was final he married the woman I'd caught him in bed with. The same woman he had at the reunion even after telling me he wouldn't be there."

Another catch in her throat had to be dealt with before she could deliver the coup de grâce. "Of course he had to know that if he'd told me he *was* going I wouldn't have, and if I hadn't gone, I wouldn't have been able to see that his new wife was pregnant. Tricking me into that was at least as low—if not lower—than finding him in bed with her."

"He didn't really do that," Ben said in disbelief. "Knowing how much you wanted a baby—"

"'Fraid so," Clair said, trying to make light of it. "He apparently needed me to see that the cause of our not having one wasn't him."

"Bastard."

"That came as a big shock to me," Clair said by way of agreement. "To be with someone from the time we were both kids really gave me the illusion that I knew him. But I *so* didn't know him. And not only when it came to his having an affair I never thought he would have. The divorce was…a nightmare."

"Are there any that aren't?"

"I think some are worse than others. Mine, in particular, was brutal. And costly."

"Legal fees?" Ben asked with a furrowed brow.

"Yes, but more than that. The other thing about Rob that I hadn't realized before was—" Clair paused. "I'm not sure how to put it…. It never occurred to me how grasping he could be. That he was so determined not to give up anything to me. I think if he could have had me leave with nothing but the clothes on my back he still would have felt as if I was getting away with something I shouldn't have. I guess that the same way he needed to flaunt his affair and take my dignity, he also had that same kind of drive to take away everything else."

Ben didn't say anything to that. He merely shook his head and continued to comfort her through that massage of her hand.

"I don't know," Clair said then. "I genuinely thought Rob was the one person I never had to worry about being vulnerable to. And instead, he was the person I should have been the most worried about."

"He had the power to hurt you the most," Ben said gently.

"A power I don't want anyone else to have over me ever again in any way."

Ben reared back slightly at that. "Wow," he said in response to the vehemence in her statement. "That's pretty extreme. How can you possibly keep *anyone* from *ever* having the power to hurt you again in any way?"

"It's just how I feel. Protective, I guess. Of myself and of…what I care about. I've lost a lot in the last year."

"Your dad, your husband—"

"The person I thought was my best friend and my soul mate—as corny as that sounds—and everything else that Rob could get, including half of my goldfish," she finished with a humorless little laugh over that last part.

"He even took your goldfish?"

"And he didn't like them or take care of them. But he had to have them just so I couldn't."

"You're making me want to wake up the owner of the pet store right now so I can buy you a fish."

That made her laugh with more humor. "I bought myself replacements for the three he got custody of. It was just the principle of the thing and the fact that—as dumb as it may sound—I really loved all of my goldfish."

"So you honestly did lose a lot," Ben said then. "When you look at it like that it's no wonder you're feeling the need to protect yourself."

And to protect, and possibly keep for herself alone, the baby she would finally have.

"And since then?" he asked. "Have you dated?"

She assumed he meant besides that night they'd spent together at the reunion and any time they'd spent together since she'd been in Northbridge.

"I've been asked out by a few of the single dads at the day care, but I haven't gone," she answered.

"So you've had the chance but you've chosen not to."

That seemed important to him.

"Right."

"And then there was the reunion where you had a lot to get back at the golden boy for."

"If you mean that the way it sounds, you're wrong," she said, surprised to hear that perspective on the night they'd spent together. "I did not use you to get back at Rob, if that's what you're implying."

"It's okay. I couldn't blame you. He had it coming. He had more than that coming."

"But that isn't what happened," she insisted.

"No?"

"No," Clair said fervently. "When I saw Rob and his

new wife I just wanted to leave. But Cassie talked me out of it and then sent you to keep me company, which I didn't even know she was arranging until you showed up at my table. I'll admit Rob was on my mind at that point and through part of the first margarita, but in case you've missed it somewhere along the way, you can be quite a diversion."

"Can I?" he said as if he were challenging that notion, even though, in the light of the moon, she could see him smile just enough to let her know it pleased him to hear it.

"As I recall," she said, "there was laughing and joking and a not insubstantial helping of charm being thrown around. Plus you aren't altogether hard on the eyes, and by the second margarita I was not thinking about Rob anymore."

"What were you thinking about?"

"Not Rob," she repeated more earnestly.

But Ben wasn't going to let it go at that. "What, then?" he persisted.

She wasn't thrilled with the idea of telling him the specifics. But the last thing she wanted him to believe was that she'd used him. So she conceded.

"I was thinking about what amazing eyes you have, for one," she said. "And that when you looked at me it was as if you didn't know there was anyone else in the room. Which seemed only fair since I was having trouble remembering there was anyone else in the place, too," she added quietly.

"Are you lyin' to cover your tracks?" he demanded but with a hint of teasing that let her know that if he doubted her, it wasn't completely.

"So I'm a person who uses people and lies, too? You think very highly of me, don't you?" she said sharply.

"Nah," he countered in a hurry and with force. "I didn't mean that. I guess I'm just being a little self-protective, too."

He used the hand that held hers to pull her down to him, to meet her eyes with those amazing ones of his as something changed between them suddenly.

"This is your last night here, you know?" he said then in a huskier voice.

"I know."

"I'm not liking it that much," he confessed. "That wouldn't be true if I thought unkindly of you."

"It might. I've always heard that bad boys like bad girls."

That made him laugh a rich, sexy laugh. "It isn't that kind of bad they like."

"Oh? What kind of bad is it?"

He merely smiled his devil's smile and it was the only answer she got as he studied her face with eyes that seemed to see more than the surface.

Somewhere along the way his arms had come around her and now the hand that had been holding hers, the hand that had pulled her down to him, went to cup the back of her head, to ease her closer still so he could kiss her. So she could kiss him.

Because that's what she did. Even knowing that she shouldn't.

But it *was* her last night with him—that was what she kept thinking. Her last time with him. Maybe her last time with him *ever.* Certainly the last time with him that would be like this.

And she wanted just this one more time with him like this—having him kiss her with lips only beginning to part, to hint that there was more to come. With his muscular arms around her. With his hands in her hair, his fingers massaging her scalp, testing the short springy curls.

She wanted just this last time with him that was so different than any other time with anyone else.

And so she kissed him back. She let her lips part in answer to his. She met his tongue when it came to greet hers. She let one of her hands go to the side of his neck while the other went to his chest. And she allowed herself to merely float without thought of anything but how this man could make her feel.

And oh, but he made her feel wonderful.

He managed to roll so that she was on her back then and he was lying beside her, partially over her as their kiss gained intensity. His mouth opened more, his tongue did a delicious dance with hers, and the hand that had found its way to her bare shoulder kneaded it in a vivid reminder of what that same hand had done to her breast the night before.

Breasts that remembered his touch too well and yearned for it again. That felt as if they were swelling with need as her nipples grew taut and seemed to scream for attention.

Attention she also had the urge to pay him.

She pulled his shirttails from his waistband and slid both hands underneath to his back. To the broad expanse of male body that widened from narrow waist to massive shoulders. Smooth and sleek—it was like solid rock worn slippery by water and wind.

Craving more still, she withdrew from under his shirt and made him groan in complaint even as his mouth possessed hers. But the complaint ceased when she reached for the buttons of his shirt, unfastened them and slid it off.

With his chest bare, Clair pressed her palms to it, traveling over bulging pectorals, finding his nipples feebly imitating hers and taunting them just a little.

His hand moved from her shoulder then, making a short trek to the back of her neck where her halter dress was held fast by two buttons.

Two buttons that came loose almost instantly.

The dress was free-flowing from there—a well-designed A-line that had skimmed her body and now provided no resistance as Ben slipped it completely off.

Of course Clair didn't provide any resistance, either, accommodating the few maneuverings required to be left in nothing but her lace panties.

But still he didn't give her what she wanted most at that moment—he didn't reach for her breasts. It was his own button and fly he attended to, shedding his jeans so they could join her discarded dress. Returning to send her panties on their way, too.

And then he was back from the brief separation required for it all, his body following the length of hers while mouths and tongues ravaged each other with wicked abandon and his hand finally found the straining, engorged globe of her breast.

It felt so incredible she couldn't help arching off the ground, writhing into his grip as he worked much greater wonders there than he had at her shoulder.

Kisses became hot and hungry and urgent, and then hardly like kisses at all.

His hand tended one breast and then the other, kneading, finding her nipples with his flattened palm, with his fingertips—tugging, teasing, tracing the sensitive outer circle until she was so tight it nearly pinched and then starting all over again until he'd worked her into such a frenzy her head fell back, away from his.

Ben kissed a hot path down the column of her throat, flicking the tip of his tongue into the hollow, sliding it along the rim of her collarbone and leaving a moist trail to chill-dry in the dark night that cloaked them in a special privacy all their own.

He kissed her shoulder. He nuzzled her arm with his nose. He gently nipped the tender flesh just above her breast and then finished the journey to take her nipple into his mouth.

But just barely at first. Tormenting her with the need

for more. Flicking the very crest with his tongue so slightly that it raised a torturous need for more.

Then more was what he gave. He drew her breast deeply into the majesty of that mouth, doing with his tongue and teeth what his fingers had done moments earlier. And all while his hand went on a journey of its own.

Down her still-flat belly. Across to her hip. Southward on her thigh. Around to the inside of that thigh. Up again…

Clair's spine arched once more when he reached the soft, sweet juncture of her body. And she couldn't help moaning when he found the very center of it and came inside. Moaning again when he drew out and forward to drive her nearly wild.

Wild enough to lose herself in the sensations, to want nothing but more of them. More of him.

Once again her hands went traveling, coursing down his back to his taut rear end where one hand remained while she drew the other around to the front of him.

Finding that part of him that was long, thick, hard…

This time Ben groaned with pleasure and writhed for her.

But only briefly before he deserted her breast to bring his entire, magnificent body above her. To fit himself between her thighs. To find that core of her again with more than his fingers, easing into her until they were completely joined, once again—like that night at the reunion—too carried away to remember protection.

His mouth rediscovered hers, wide-open and lazy as

he began to move within her. Slowly, carefully, every movement seeming calculated and controlled for the best effect. And the best effects were what he elicited.

Gradually, he picked up the pace, thrusting his tongue the same way—in and out—keeping a close rhythm above and below, a pace, a rhythm she could answer as together they worked toward that greater goal. As bodies met and melded. As pulses seemed to beat in unison. As every nerve ending rose to the surface, aware, alert, alive.

In and out. Faster and faster, until Clair couldn't keep up. Until the best she could do was flex and release muscles and cling to his powerful back, opening to him, welcoming him, tightening around him, reveling in the feel of him full and deep within her.

And then it began. Like a bud in the very center of her. A bright and sparkling bud. Awakening. Coming to life. Reaching, striving, working for the warmth, the brightness of the sun.

Ben found it for them both and Clair burst into that radiant release her body needed so desperately. She held fast to the steely strength of his body above hers as wave after wave of the most exquisite bliss coursed through her, carrying her to the very heart of that shared moment of unparalleled pleasure and leaving her, leaving Ben, breathlessly entwined and molded each to the other.

For a time they stayed that way, until hearts were beating normally again and breathing came easier. Then Ben raised up on his elbows. Cupping her head in his hands, he kissed her—softly but with a passion not completely spent.

"You leave me speechless," he whispered when he'd finished kissing her.

"Then don't talk," she advised as she gazed up into that handsome face.

He took the advice and instead slipped out of her, rolling to his back and bringing her with him to lie against his side.

That was where they remained—her head cradled in the dip of his shoulder, her palm resting on his chest, his arms wrapped around her, holding her close—as he slowly succumbed to sleep.

And as Clair laid there she consciously held on to that moment in time, savoring the feel of his nakedness against hers; the sound of his steady, strong pulse beneath her ear; the heat of his body infusing hers; the way his arms seamlessly circled her, his elbow resting just above her abdomen where his baby grew….

It was all just so nice.

So, so nice.

And she had to fight hard not to wish—just a little—that it could last….

Chapter Eight

Ben stood at the sliding glass door in the kitchen the next morning while he had his first cup of coffee. But it wasn't the sight of the blazing sunshine he was intent on. It wasn't the sight of the barn door that needed painting or the brick pavers waiting to be replaced in the patio. He was staring at the cottage.

And his mind was on Clair.

They'd spent most of the night on the blanket next to the stream. After a nap, they'd made love a second time with even more passion, even more abandon, even more intensity, before he'd brought her home.

He'd almost gone in with her and initiated a third round of lovemaking but by then he could see that she was really—*really*—tired and so after a few kisses at her door that had made it tougher than hell to leave, he'd turned her by the shoulders and sent her inside alone.

Then he'd gone to his own lonely bed and struggled to sleep when what he'd wanted so damn bad was to be with her. To have her snuggled up to him. To have her sleeping in his arms even if she hadn't been up to making love again.

And that's what had him thinking this morning.

That and the fact that she was leaving today.

To go all the way back to Denver.

And not only wouldn't he have any more nights like last night with her, he wouldn't have anything else with her, either.

It shouldn't have mattered—that's what he kept telling himself. Okay, so they'd had a great night together at the reunion, a great week together since she'd been back, another more-than-great night together last night. That didn't mean anything except that they'd had some good times. He should chalk it up to just that, accept that that's all there was to it, and put it behind him. Get on with his life and the business at hand—opening the school.

But regardless of how many times he told himself that, he just couldn't seem to do it. He couldn't seem to accept that that was all there was, all there would ever be, between them.

He couldn't accept it because that wasn't the way he wanted it to be.

That bit of revelation was difficult for him to admit. It meant that in spite of all his warnings to himself, his determination not to get involved with a woman on the rebound—not to be the rebound guy for anyone ever again—he'd done it anyway.

And this time he hadn't even done it blindly, the way he had with Heather. This time he'd known going in—or at least going into this past week—that Clair was fresh out of a marriage and that people who were newly single were *not* a good bet for any kind of serious relationship. But still he'd let himself get in deeper and deeper with her.

What did that make him? Stupid beyond belief?

Maybe.

But stupid or not, he was in pretty deep if he couldn't stand the thought of her leaving today.

And he couldn't.

So, how much trouble was he in? he wondered.

As far as feelings went? He had an inkling that he was definitely in trouble.

She was on his mind all the time—*all* the time. She was the first thing he thought about when he woke up in the morning. She was the last thing he thought about at night when he went to sleep. She was there in his thoughts constantly through the day, whether he was with her or not—wondering about her, wondering if she would like this or that, approve of this or that, what she would think, what she would say, how soon he could talk to her, how soon he could see her, be with her again, make the time he was with her last.

And through it all, he *cared*. He cared what would happen when they got together for the day. He cared how the day had gone at the end of it. He cared what she was doing, whether he was with her or not, who she was with, if she was having a better time without him, whether she was having a good time if she was with him. He cared that she might disapprove of some-thing—anything. He cared what she might think. What she might say. He sure as hell cared how long it would be before he got to see her again and he wanted what-ever time he had with her to go on and on.

And not only did he care, she had an impact on him in every way. The sound of her voice was enough to give him the sense that all was right with the world. The sight of her seemed to be the only thing he needed to brighten the worst day. Making her laugh thrilled him—it actu-ally gave him a charge. Touching her made his blood rush faster through his veins.

And every single second he wasn't with her, he wanted to be.

But Clair *was* fresh out of a marriage—there was no way around that, he reminded himself, trying hard to keep his head on straight, to keep some perspective.

And she hadn't had any other relationships since get-ting out of that marriage. That made him the first. That made him the rebound guy. That made him exactly what he'd never wanted to be again.

The guy who got left behind.

Even Cassie had said that she wouldn't have set him

up with Clair now. That it would be different if it was two years from now and Clair was healed and over her divorce, but not now. Which meant that his sister didn't think Clair was ready for a relationship and Cassie probably knew Clair better than anyone.

Although, on the other hand, he thought, Clair *was* a little further along than Heather had been. He'd hooked up with Heather the same day her divorce had become final. She hadn't even caught her breath.

Clair had a little more distance from her divorce than that. At least the dust had settled before they'd gotten together at the reunion. And here they were, almost three months later. Three months further away from it. Three months longer for her to have healed and adjusted and gotten back on track.

Plus, Clair might not have had any other relationships since her divorce, but she had been asked out—that meant that unlike Heather, Clair had had some confirmation that she was still attractive and desirable. That had been a big part of the service he'd provided for Heather—boosting her ego, bolstering her self-confidence, reminding her that she could still attract a man's attention, interest, admiration. Clair had to already know she was capable of that.

So, those were positives, weren't they? That even if she hadn't had a lot of time since her divorce she had had some? And that even if she hadn't had a real rebound relationship yet, she'd at least had some validation?

Or was he just grasping at straws?

He might be grasping at straws to some degree. But he had a lot riding on this suddenly and he had to take what he could get in the way of reassuring himself that he might have a chance to make this work out with her.

A chance to make this work out with her?

That echoed in his mind as the other reason he'd initially set out not to let anything happen came back to him.

The school. The school was a big deal to him. A huge deal to him. The school was something he needed not to be distracted from. Something he didn't want to be distracted from. Something that required, that deserved, all his energies, his attention, his focus.

And it didn't get all his energies, his attention or his focus when a large portion of those were going to Clair. When a large portion of them would go to her in the future if he didn't cut things off with her right now.

Of course she'd made her own contribution to the school, too. To be fair, he couldn't discount that. She'd been as much of a help to him since she'd been in Northbridge as she'd been a distraction.

And she could go on being a help, if she was around. She could be even more of a help than she'd already been. After all, she *had* finished her growing-up years right there at the school, which meant that she knew the ins and outs of running the place. Plus she ran an entire day-care center herself—there was value in that experience.

So maybe if she was around more, it wouldn't be the

way it might be if someone else were distracting him because she could be an asset in her own right, and it would all balance.

If she was around more.

If she was around at all.

If she didn't try to slip out the way she had the morning after the reunion.

Was that why he was standing there at the door, watching? To make sure she didn't disappear again before he knew it?

If that was the reason, it wasn't a good sign. He shouldn't even be considering a relationship with someone he couldn't rely on.

Was Clair unreliable? Was that why he was standing there watching the cottage?

Clair—unreliable…

He tried that on for size. But it just didn't fit. It felt more in line with the exchange he and Clair had had the night before when she'd accused him of considering her to be a person who lied and used other people, of not thinking very highly of her.

He'd known the minute she'd said that that it was his own old baggage. That it had had almost nothing to do with Clair.

Clair didn't use people the way Heather had used him. After that conversation he'd had with Clair last night he'd thought back on the reunion, on the way things had been before they'd ended up at her room at the bed-and-breakfast. She could have flaunted him in front of her ex, she could have fallen all over him so her ex would have been witness to it.

But she hadn't done any of that. He hadn't even known her former husband and his pregnant new wife were there. Clair had kept being with him low-key and unobtrusive.

And as for lying? She could have tried to make up something to excuse her abrupt departure the morning after the reunion, or she could have put the blame on him—she could have said he'd done something wrong, something offensive, something that had caused her to leave without a word.

But she hadn't. She'd owned up to it. She'd been candid about how confused she'd felt that next morning. About the fact that she'd never done anything like spend the night with a stranger before and had been at a loss as to how to act—that was all about as honest as anyone could be expected to be.

Of course she *had* run out in the first place.

But he had to admit that that hadn't been on his mind when he'd first come to the kitchen door to look at the cottage and drink his coffee. It hadn't been a concern to him. It hadn't even occurred to him until now. And even now he didn't actually think she was on the verge of sneaking out to her car at any moment. The thought had just been a flash of his own paranoia.

No, Clair wasn't unreliable, and he knew it. In fact, she was all the more impressive because she'd forged through her own embarrassment over what had happened in June to come back here and help him with the school when she could have just refused.

The truth was, there just wasn't anything about Clair that he wasn't bowled over by. That he didn't like. That he didn't more than like.

Except that she hadn't been out of her marriage for long.

But as he stood there, picturing her, remembering what it had been like to hold her, to kiss her, to make love to her, he knew he couldn't merely sit by and watch her leave today just because he might be the rebound guy. He knew he couldn't watch her walk out of his life and not even try for more.

He had too many feelings—strong feelings—for her. Feelings that were worth the effort. Worth the risk.

He just had to hope that what had been between them from the moment they met was in spite of how she'd been hurt before.

And not just the first step out of it.

Clair was sound asleep when a knock on the cottage door startled her awake. Or partially awake, anyway. For a split second she thought she was back on the blanket beside the stream and she wondered where there could be a door for anyone to knock on and why anyone would be knocking on a door beside a stream. And where Ben was…

Ben.

The thought of him brought her completely awake.

Awake enough to remember that he'd taken her home just before dawn and left her at her door even though she would have rather he'd come in to her bed with her.

Awake enough to recall that he'd said he couldn't do that and not make love to her again, but that he thought she'd better get some rest instead.

Was he back now that she'd had some rest? To make love to her?

"Come in! It's open," she called a bit dreamily before she'd considered that it might not be Ben who was knocking. Or that if it was Ben, she shouldn't be so ready, so eager, to make love with him again without even thinking about it.

But still, the moment she heard the door open, her eyes flew open, too, and with a voice full of hope she said, "Ben?"

There was no answer. But the cottage was small and within moments he was there, at her bedroom door, freshly showered and shaved, wearing a pair of jeans and a gray T-shirt stretched taut across his pectorals and biceps.

Pectorals and biceps she wanted to run her hands all over…again.

"It is you," she said, more to herself than to him, almost a purr.

"Who else would it be?" he asked with a mischievous smile.

"One of my other bridge-side lotharios," she countered, shamelessly happy to see him even as she began to realize that she *had* been so tired by the time she'd gotten in this morning that she'd had a very quick shower and slipped into bed in nothing but a pair of panties.

"One of your other bridge-side lotharios?" he repeated with an even bigger grin that hiked up one side of his supple mouth more than the other. "Do you have a lot of them?"

"Only three or four," she countered as she eased herself to sit against the headboard, careful to keep the sheet held above her breasts by one hand and wishing at least mascara had magically applied itself while she'd slept.

"Maybe I shouldn't be seen, though," she said then, using her free hand to fluff her hair slightly, counting her blessings that the curls didn't look too much different when she got up in the morning than they did after she'd brushed them out and arranged them.

"Let's see," he said, pretending to take stock as he crossed the room and sat on the edge of the bed, facing her. "You look all pink-cheeked and clean-faced…" He leaned over and pressed a kiss to her naked shoulder. "You smell terrific, and you've inspired my curiosity about what is—or isn't—behind that sheet. I'd say you can be seen."

Clair was too busy enjoying the tiny ripples that shoulder-kiss had sent through her to worry anymore about how she looked.

"I came to talk to you," he said then.

Talking did not have the same appeal as what she'd

thought he'd come for. "You woke me up to *talk?*" she complained.

That made him smile yet again. "Well, at least at first."

"This better be good," she said in mock warning.

"I think it is. I think it's great."

"Something with the school? You've had a surge of registrations and have a wait-list before you've even opened your doors? Social services has already given you commendations for the cleanest trash receptacles in the state? You were planting a tree in the yard and struck oil? What?"

"Not something to do with the school. Something to do with you and me."

That seemed intriguing but she had no other guesses for what he was there to tell her that had to do with them both so she simply said, "What to do with you and me?"

"I left you here last night and regretted it."

"Regretted what we did earlier by the bridge? Or leaving me here to go to bed alone?" Clair said, still not taking this too seriously, thinking he was playing around as a segue to making love again.

"I did *not* regret what we did by the bridge," he said, grinning.

He took her free hand in both of his, cocooning it and making her want to feel his touch everywhere else.

Then he said, "I regretted leaving you here."

"You could have stayed," she reminded him.

"I spent the rest of the night wishing I had. And tossing and turning because I hadn't. Then I got up this morning and came to some conclusions."

"Conclusions?" she repeated.

"I hate the thought of you going back to Denver. Today or ever," he announced.

Her thinking was still stuck on the school and their connection through it. "You'll do fine. You're on top of everything around here. You didn't even really need me to do what I did—I was more moral support than anything. Besides, you've worked with kids like you'll have, you know what you're doing and you have a good staff coming in to help."

"I told you, this isn't about the school. I'm talking about you and me—although I did think it would be terrific to have you working here. But that wasn't what motivated this. I don't want you to go back to Denver because I want us to be together. Like last night. Only long-term."

"Oh," she said as she finally began to switch gears and omit the school from her thinking.

He really was talking about the two of them. As a couple. Getting together. Being together.

Long-term…

She didn't know exactly what *long-term* meant. Or even exactly what being together entailed. But for a moment it was still enough to spark an old fantasy. An old fantasy in which she was married, having a baby, having the whole storybook life she'd always wanted.

But it was an old fantasy.

An old fantasy that had exploded in her face.

"Oh," she said again, this time ominously.

"Look, I know this is quick. I know the ink is barely dry on your divorce papers—believe me, it was my biggest hurdle. But the ink *is* dry, and you're free to move on. To start over."

But to her, moving on and starting over had meant being on her own. It had meant being self-sufficient. Self-reliant. It had meant taking care of herself, protecting herself. Keeping herself emotionally safe by not opening up to another man. By not letting another man get close enough to her to wreak the kind of havoc Rob had.

Another man like Ben, who sat there looking so handsome, so sexy that she had to fight the urge to throw her arms around him and agree to anything he wanted just to be with him.

But that urge alone was proof that she was already more vulnerable to him than she wanted to be. Than she'd wanted to be to anyone ever again.

"I have moved on and started over," she said, hearing the chilly defiance that had come into her voice.

"So move on and start over once more," he suggested. "With me this time."

With him…

With Ben who made her feel things not even Rob had. With Ben who was a more incredible man than Rob had ever been. With Ben who was the father of her baby…

But what if she did move on and start over again with Ben? What if long-term for them meant a second marriage for her? And then what if that second marriage ended, too?

Merely thinking about that brought on vivid memories of the pain that had nearly wiped her out only months ago. She felt again the devastation. The helplessness—like drowning and not being able to find a foothold. She recalled too much of the loss, too many of the battles with Rob over everything.

She pulled her hand away from Ben's and clutched the sheet with that one, too, even more firmly than she had been.

"I know," he said softly before she said anything else, setting those hands she'd shunned on her thigh and squeezing comfortingly. "Your divorce was ugly. You were hurt and the idea of getting anywhere near anything that could cause you that kind of misery again scares the hell out of you. I understand it because I don't want a second taste of what I went through after Heather dumped me, either. Plus right now you look like a deer caught in headlights, so I know how terrified you are. But try to see past those headlights, Clair. To me."

She saw past the headlights to him. And what she saw was a strong, determined man. A man who wouldn't be set off course when he had a goal to reach. A man who had taken his teenage experiences, decided how his treatment should have been different and worked tirelessly until he'd accomplished owning his own school to do things his own way.

And he as right, she *was* terrified. Terrified of even

considering how that kind of strength and determination and tenacity might translate into actions he might take against her if things between them didn't work out. Actions he might take against her in regards to their child. And how much it could ultimately cost her.

She felt her head shake all on its own, as if her subconscious was rejecting what he was suggesting even before she'd come to it consciously, shrinking from the very possibility of the pain that could potentially result from trying again to have that fantasy storybook life.

"Come on," he cajoled in response to her head shake. "Don't let the fear win. I would never hurt you the way golden boy did."

No, Ben could hurt her even worse. He just didn't know it.

And then something awful happened.

Suddenly Clair felt a familiar warmth flow from her.

"Are you all right?" Ben asked, apparently seeing something reflected in her expression. "Are you dizzy again? Do you feel like you're going to pass out?"

She wasn't dizzy, and she didn't feel like she was going to pass out, but it did suddenly cross her mind that despite the fact that the doctor had said the dizzy spells were nothing, maybe the doctor had been wrong. Maybe they'd been a sign that things with the baby weren't right. That she was going to lose it. That she was losing it right now.

"I have to get up!" she said, still clutching the sheet to her but sitting forward, intent on leaving that bed, on running to the bathroom to see if what she was afraid was happening really was. "Move! Please! I have to get up!"

Maybe the rapid rise of panic in her voice inspired him to do as she'd asked. Ben stood in a hurry and yanked the sheet from where it was moored between the mattress and box springs so she could take it with her to run for the bathroom.

"Are you going to be sick?" he called after her.

Clair didn't answer him. She couldn't. Her heart was in her throat as she closed the bathroom door behind her, dropped the sheet and nearly tore her panties pulling them down.

"No!" she whispered when she discovered the small smudge of blood. "No! No! No!"

But as hot tears sprang to her eyes she had to hope that maybe it wasn't too late, that maybe if she could get help her baby could be saved.

"I need to get to the hospital," she called through the door, pulling a pair of pajama pants and a matching tank top from the hook on the back of it.

"The hospital?" Ben said as she was wrenching on the pajama pants, his tone confused and edged with an urgency of his own now. "What's wrong? What's going on?"

"I have to get to the hospital *right* now!" she insisted.

"Why? Tell me what's going on," he demanded, still through the door.

She didn't have time to make up a lie and at that moment nothing else seemed important anyway, so she said, "I didn't know if I was going to tell you at all, but I definitely wasn't going to tell you like this…"

"Whatever it is, just tell me!"

Dressed now, she opened the door, finding Ben looking as worried as she felt. "I'm… That night we spent together at the reunion… I'm pregnant."

"Pregnant?" he repeated as if it wasn't a word he recognized. Then light dawned. "A baby? *My* baby?"

"Yes," she confirmed, fighting not to cry. "But I'm spotting, and I'm afraid… I need to get to the hospital! Now!"

Chapter Nine

"Reid says this can be a pretty common occurrence early in a pregnancy," Cassie was saying to Clair two hours later.

Cassie had been arriving at the school just as Ben was rushing Clair to the hospital. When she'd learned what was happening, she'd followed in her own car and had been lending Clair moral support ever since by staying with her while Ben was exiled to the waiting room.

After being examined by a nurse-midwife and having an ultrasound, there didn't seem to be cause for concern, and Cassie was merely reiterating it to reassure Clair and put her fears to rest that no information was being withheld from her to keep her calm.

"Reid talked to your doctor in Denver, and he agreed that there's no cause for alarm, that you just need to take it easy for a few days—which means I get to keep you in Northbridge a little while longer," Cassie ended on a cheery note.

But Clair knew it was forced cheer. Not that she doubted that Cassie was glad for more time with her. It was just that the entire situation had come as such a shock to her friend and the stress level was running high all the way around.

Still, Clair went along with what her friend was saying and matched her tone. "You definitely seem to be stuck with me. I can't drive back to Denver alone until I'm sure nothing's going wrong. But the spotting already looks like it's stopped, so I don't think it'll be long before I get the okay."

"And then what?" Cassie ventured, her cheeriness wavering and a concerned expression peeking out from behind it as she sat in the visitor's chair beside the emergency room bed Clair still occupied while release papers were being readied.

"Yeah, I guess the cat's out of the bag, isn't it?" Clair said.

Nothing had been discussed—not with Ben as he'd driven silently to the hospital, and not with Cassie who Clair hadn't actually had the chance to talk to for any great length between doctors, nurses and technicians going in and out since she'd arrived.

But now that there seemed to be a lull, Cassie said,

"I can't believe you and Ben got together at the reunion and neither of you told me."

"It was complicated," Clair hedged.

"I feel kind of stupid horning in on the two of you every chance I got this last week when you probably wanted to be alone."

"You weren't *horning in*," Clair said in a hurry.

She had hoped to avoid getting into all the details of her own abrupt departure the morning after the reunion and the course things had taken with Ben since she'd been back in Northbridge, but she felt she owed her friend. She didn't want Cassie feeling like a fool or thinking that there was a conspiracy of sorts to keep something from her. So Clair filled her in—complete with the fact that she'd hoped getting to know Ben would help her decide what to do from here.

"Did getting to know him help you decide what to do from here?" Cassie asked when Clair concluded with that.

"No," Clair confessed. "In some ways it made me more afraid to let him know about the baby. He's just so strong-willed and determined when he sets his mind to something, and I've been so, well, I don't exactly think straight when I'm around him. I'd put off making any kind of decisions until I got home and had a clearer perspective. But then I was so scared that I was losing the baby that I just blurted it out."

Cassie frowned in confusion. "Why is Ben being strong-willed and determined a bad thing?"

"What if what he set his mind to was to getting custody of the baby?" Clair said.

"Oh, Clair," Cassie murmured, shaking her head. "You're stuck in divorce mode, aren't you? Who-gets-what-and-who-loses-it-in-the-process."

Clair didn't deny it, she merely shrugged.

For a moment Cassie didn't say anything and Clair had the impression her friend was weighing her words. Or maybe what she was weighing was the wisdom in keeping her thoughts to herself. But after a moment Clair had the impression that her friend had decided to speak her mind anyway.

"Okay," Cassie said, "I'm sure it's normal to be in the who-gets-what-and-who-loses-it-in-the-process frame of mind when you've just gone through splitting up the dishes and forks and knives—"

"And everything else."

"And everything else," Cassie conceded. "And unfortunately it supports Ben's theory about not getting involved with someone too newly divorced, and brings me back to what I ended up thinking when I suggested on Friday that you and Ben might have hit it off. You *are* still raw from your breakup with Rob. But with a baby due maybe you need to fast-forward a little through this part of your divorce recovery."

"Fast-forward through this part of my divorce recovery?" Clair said.

"Normally time would take care of this. I came away from Friday figuring that's all you needed—time—and you wouldn't be so gun-shy. That you would come around to trusting men again and wouldn't feel panicked about even the idea of someone else getting married—like you did when that woman at work got engaged. In fact, I was so sure that eventually you'd get over this that I thought I'd just watch for signs of it and then lure you back to Northbridge again to get you and Ben together after all—when he wouldn't feel like rebound boy and you'd be open to what a truly terrific guy he is. But now there's a baby and time is at a premium."

"So you think I should fast-forward," Clair reminded.

"Yes."

"And be open to what a truly terrific guy Ben is."

"He is, you know," Cassie said.

"You think he's the horse I should get back up on," Clair countered, referring to the metaphor her friend had used when they'd talked on Friday.

Cassie couldn't suppress a smile that looked just like the mischievous one Ben flashed every now and then. "I'm betting you've already done that since I overheard someone say that spotting like you've been having can be caused by vigorous lovemaking."

That *was* what the nurse-midwife had told her. But Clair couldn't help the blush that heated her cheeks at hearing that her friend had an inkling of how she'd spent the previous night.

"Uh-huh," Cassie said knowingly. "That's what I thought—you two did a replay of the reunion. So obviously I was right about there being an attraction. And now you're having a baby together. To me that means we need to get you both past the obstacles standing in your way."

Hurdles—that was what Ben had said, Clair recalled. That he'd already gotten over his.

Although he could clearly have developed some new ones with what he'd learned this morning….

Cassie was continuing to make her point though. "So yes, I think my brother is a truly terrific guy and that you should fast-forward to opening your eyes to that."

"I'm sure he is a terrific guy——"

"No, you're not if you think for a single second that he would do anything to take away your baby."

"Custody battles happen all the time. And even if it didn't come to that completely, there's still *shared* custody, which would mean I'd lose half——"

"Stop," Cassie said flatly. "Again, you're in divorce mode, splitting things up. Get out of it."

Clair didn't say anything to that.

"I want you to just open your eyes to Ben, period," Cassie ordered. "And to how you feel about him—separate from the fears and distrust you have left over from the divorce. *Fast-forward,*" Cassie repeated emphatically. "Pretend it's been another year or two, and you've looked around and seen that there are a lot of good guys out there, a lot of marriages that work, a lot of people who are happy together—forever. And you're beginning to realize that there's no reason you can't be one of them. That you can't have one of the good guys, have a marriage that works, and be happy with someone forever. *That's* when I would have set you up with my brother."

"I don't know, Cassie."

"You know you're attracted enough to him to have slept with him—at the reunion and again this trip. And I know you and, knowing you, I know that there has to be something there, some part of you that actually does trust him, for that to have happened."

"Maybe Ben's right and it's just some rebound thing."

"Is it?" Cassie demanded.

Clair considered that. But in considering it she thought about what had gotten her into bed with him both times and she knew it wasn't because she was looking for any kind of validation that she could still attract a man. Both times it had been all about just wanting to be with him, wanting to get her hands on him, to have his hands on her. It had been about wanting him.

"No," she admitted. "I don't think it's a rebound thing."

"Then figure out what it is and work from there," Cassie ordered.

The nurse came in just then with the release papers for Clair to sign. While Clair did that Cassie remained on the sidelines.

Then the nurse said Clair was free to dress and go home, and left, and Cassie stood to give her friend the privacy to do that.

But before she did, she said, "I'm not hanging around here to get in the middle of things with you and Ben. But I'm counting on you to do that fast-forwarding, Clair. Rob may have taken a lot away from you but don't let him have taken the opportunity for you to be happy with someone else. Especially when that someone else is the father of the baby you're going to have. The father of my niece or nephew."

Again Clair didn't have a response so she merely said, "I don't think Ben will kick me out of the cottage yet, do you?"

"He's already told Reid you'll go on staying there and that he'll sleep on the couch so he'll be within shouting distance if anything starts up again."

The possibility of having Ben in the cottage with her might have given Clair a bit of titillation except that she wasn't sure how angry or disgusted he might be with her. Or where this turn of events had left them. So instead the idea of being alone with him only made her tense.

"Maybe you can come out later, then?" she said hopefully.

"I will, but not without calling first to make sure I don't walk in on something I don't want to walk in on," Cassie said, regaining a hint of humor in her tone.

Cassie left then and Clair didn't hesitate to get out of the hospital bed—although she did it gingerly, in spite of all the reassurances she'd had that the baby was doing fine.

Her friend had folded her clothes and set them on the

countertop that was just outside of the curtain that had been pulled around her bed so—holding the back of the hospital gown closed—she went out from behind the curtain to retrieve them.

Above the counter and the supply cabinets and drawers it rested atop were windows that afforded a view of the bullpen where emergency room staff were either writing in charts or using the telephone or the computers. Beyond that Clair could see a portion of the waiting room.

She could see Ben.

He was standing at a wall of windows himself, but Clair knew that his view from there was of the parking lot, which couldn't compare with her view of him.

Tall and straight and sturdy, he stood in profile, one arm raised high, his forearm against the glass, his brow resting against that forearm.

Clearly he was troubled or worried or angry or all three—it wasn't a carefree, happy posture—and Clair felt a combination of things herself to see it.

She was sorry that this was the way he'd found out about the baby. She was concerned about what damage finding out like this had done to their relationship— whatever that relationship was. And there was a part of her that was afraid he hated the fact that there was going to be a baby at all.

That part of her, of her thoughts, came as a surprise. If Ben hated that there was going to be a baby, wouldn't that give her license to leave Northbridge and him behind, license to keep the baby as hers alone? And wasn't keeping the baby as hers alone what she'd thought she wanted this whole time?

It *was* what she'd thought she wanted this whole time. But maybe it wasn't what she actually *did* want.

She took her clothes from the counter and went behind the drawn curtain again. But not looking at Ben any longer didn't erase him from her mind. He was still there, a presence that suddenly made it seem silly that she'd ever believed he could be pushed into the background, ignored and eventually forgotten about as she raised his child without him.

Of course it *had* been nice to have him with her when the spotting had begun, to know he would take care of her, get her to the hospital, make sure she received the care she needed as soon as they got there. It had been nice to know that she *wasn't* alone. To have the support of the big, strong, capable man who had fathered her baby.

And suddenly considering returning to Denver alone, having the baby alone, facing whatever complications might arise alone, raising the baby alone, took on a new magnitude. It became more real to her.

Yes, if she excluded Ben she wouldn't have to share the joys of their child, but she also wouldn't have anyone to share the things that weren't such a joy. The worries and fears and concerns and problems. And now that she'd weathered a minor storm along those lines, facing the myriad of worries and fears and concerns and problems that she knew would arise—facing them by herself—seemed more overwhelming.

Maybe she didn't want to do this on her own.

Maybe there was something to be said for sharing the not-so-good.

Maybe there was something to be said for sharing the good, too.

Clair sat on the visitor's chair to pull on her pajama pants. But once she got there, she just went on holding the soft cotton lounging slacks in her hands, staring at nothing in particular, lost in the thoughts that were racing through her head. Lost in the confusion those thoughts were causing because they were so different from what she'd been thinking since she'd learned she was pregnant. So different from what she'd been thinking since she'd found Rob in bed with someone else.

If she didn't want to have and raise this child on her own, if she wanted to share it—the good and bad—that meant an entire change of course from the one she'd embraced with such fervor since her divorce. It meant letting another man get close. As close, closer, even, than Rob had been.

It meant letting Ben get that close…

And merely entertaining the glimmer of that possibility scared her to death.

Anybody who got that close could hurt her as badly as Rob had.

It was lucky she wasn't still hooked up to the blood-pressure monitor because her heart was suddenly beating so fast and hard she could feel it, her throat felt constricted, her ears were ringing, her head was light and she felt as if she could barely breathe.

None of it was good and she knew it. She knew it couldn't be good for the baby. She knew it couldn't be conducive to keeping the spotting at bay.

She knew she had to get a grip.

She took a deep breath and blew it out slowly. Then another. Then another, until she had managed to relax, at least a little.

Divorce mode—that's what Cassie had called her current mind-set and since what she'd just felt was the same thing she'd felt on her way into the courthouse for the final divorce decree to be granted, it was a pretty sure bet that Cassie was right and divorce mode was what she was still in.

But was it possible to fast-forward through it, the way Cassie had suggested? she wondered.

Trying to find a way to do that, she adopted more of Cassie's advice and tried to imagine this was a year or two down the road.

It wasn't easy.

At first all she could think was that no matter how much time passed, she would feel the same as she felt right then about getting too close to another man. She would feel the way she'd told Cassie on Friday that she felt—like a turtle that needed to pull into its shell to protect itself.

But then she thought about this trip to Northbridge, about the people she'd met or reconnected with here, about the marriages she'd seen, about the men…

Ben's brother Ad and his wife Kit came to mind. And so did Ad's friend Cutty and his wife Kira. Both couples had been great together. They obviously loved—and liked—each other, genuinely enjoyed being with each other, were bonded in a way that seemed impenetrable.

Granted both couples were newly married, but they were happy and things seemed to be falling into place for them—Kira was adopting Cutty's twin daughters, Kit was opening her own cake shop—and Clair had felt as if their happiness together could go on forever. As if their marriages could work.

And if it could work for them, why *couldn't* it work for her?

Plus when she thought about the men here—even just the men on the Northbridge Bruisers sports team—she had to concede, too, that Cassie was right about there being a lot of good guys out there. The team itself was made up of a whole slew of men she'd known when she'd lived in Northbridge, men who had stayed and made something of themselves, made commitments they'd kept in one form or another, men even she—in her recent jaded frame of mind—still considered genuinely good guys. The Walker brothers themselves were examples of character, integrity, morals and a strong sense of loyalty.

And that included Ben.

Okay, so yes, she admitted that in spite of Ben's misdeeds as a teenager, he'd grown into a man whose strong-will and determination were poured into positive things—working his way through college and getting his degree, repaying his mother the money it had cost her to send him to Arizona, opening his own school.

That made him very different from Rob. Rob, who had always been the golden boy, who had never met any kind of adversity, and who—the first time things hadn't gone the way he'd expected them to—had only been able to deal with it by placing blame. By placing blame on Clair. By striking out against her, resenting her and ultimately punishing her.

She felt certain that in Ben's same shoes, Rob would have grown up holding a grudge against the mother who had sent him to Arizona. Rob would have made it his goal to get back at her rather than repaying her.

And by the same token, Clair knew that if she had had a child with Rob and their marriage had still dissolved, it wouldn't have only been her goldfish he'd have fought to keep from her. He would most definitely have sued her for custody or at least taken away as much of her time with their child as he possibly could have. Just out of spite.

And so she'd assumed that Ben would do the same thing if he knew there was going to be a baby.

But because Rob would have done that didn't mean Ben would. Just as Ben had made the best out of his early life experiences, and Rob had made the worst out of the difficulties of their infertility together, she realized that while Rob had willfully hurt her, that wasn't something Ben would ever do. Not when he so fiercely regretted that he'd hurt his mother and his family with his teenage antics. Not when—all these years later—he still felt guilty for it. She knew that there was no way he would purposely cause pain to anyone again after the lesson he'd learned. That when he'd said this morning that he would never hurt her, it hadn't been an idle promise or empty words, he'd meant it.

And if she could believe that, which she did, then maybe she really could trust him.

Or maybe, deep down, below the divorce debris, she'd always known she could trust him and that was why she had already trusted him enough to have slept with him—the way Cassie had suggested.

Cassie, who had also suggested that Clair just needed to open her eyes to Ben as the man he actually was, without her vision being tainted by the man Rob had proven to be.

The man Ben actually was.

Clair thought seriously about that, trying hard to see Ben through clearer eyes.

The man Ben actually was was a man who was dedicated and committed—she knew that for a fact. He was a man whose strength of character had been forged by his boyhood problems. A man who was steadfast in his determination to do what he felt was right. A man who had been honest and aboveboard even about dating Lois Erickson when he could have easily lied about it, but who hadn't thrown it in Clair's face the way Rob had thrown in her face his affair, his new marriage, his success at getting his wife pregnant.

In fact, Ben was a man who had been a whole lot more honest and aboveboard with Clair than Clair had been with him. That was a sorry fact, and she wasn't proud of it. Actually, when she looked at things from that perspective, she was ashamed of herself.

More ashamed of herself when she remembered Ben coming into the cottage to wake her up this morning. When she recalled him sitting on the edge of the bed, taking her hand, telling her that he didn't want her to go back to Denver, that he wanted them to be together. Long-term. Telling her he understood her fears of getting involved again, that he'd gotten over his own hurdles.

And all she'd done in response to that was panic.

So what now? she asked herself. Could she get over her own hurdles? And if she could, would it matter or had she gone too far? Had she angered and alienated him to such an extent that there was no hope for them?

She thought she could get over her own hurdles because she knew now that being in divorce mode had skewed her vision of almost everything. But being aware of it, she thought she could avoid it. She thought that it was like wearing sunglasses indoors—she just had to remember to take off the sunglasses. Only in this, she just had to remember that not all men were Rob Cabot and that her judgements might be shaded a bit by her experiences with him if she didn't consciously try to keep that from happening.

Besides, getting over her own hurdles was suddenly worth the effort because she also knew now that she wanted more than anything to share her baby with it's father. To share the whole experience. To give birth, to watch the baby grow, to raise it and weather all the storms with Ben.

But more than that, what she wanted was Ben himself. What she wanted was what she'd fantasized that morning, what she'd told herself was only an illusion—marriage, this baby, the whole storybook life. With Ben.

And if she'd angered and alienated him too much for any of that to be possible?

She just wouldn't accept it.

She'd own up to the fact that yes, she'd done wrong by him when she'd disappeared the morning after the reunion without a word. That yes, she'd done wrong by him when she hadn't been honest and aboveboard about the pregnancy that had resulted from that night they'd spent together.

But she would also do whatever it took to convince him that, like his early misdeeds, she wanted to put right again what she'd done wrong. She wanted to make up for it all.

She wanted him.

She just didn't know, as she finally began to dress, what it was going to take to accomplish all of that.

The drive home from the hospital was short and purely instructional. Without giving Clair the opportunity to get in a word edgewise, Ben relayed the orders his brother had given him that while Clair did not need to be confined to bed, she was to be off her feet as much as possible, that she was to lift nothing, eat and drink well and generally rest. Therefore, Ben dictated, he would set her up in the school's recreation room with the television and the remote control during the daytime hours while he worked, so he could check on her repeatedly and often. And each night when she was ready to retire, he would—as Cassie had already told Clair—sleep on the couch in the cottage's living room to be at her beck and call there, too.

"Thank you?" Clair said, unsure whether that was the correct response to the boot-camp-like indoctrination as they reached the school and Ben drove around back to the cottage.

There was nothing warm or friendly in any of what he'd said or in his clipped attitude, leaving Clair feeling more nervous by the minute about breaking through that wall of anger and alienation that she knew was her own fault.

But once they were inside the cottage again she knew she couldn't let this go on any longer. So, in the middle of his closing the door behind them as he laid out a game plan for her to shower while he made the bed, she said a quiet, "Stop."

He did. He stopped talking instantly and merely finished closing the door.

Although when he had, he didn't turn to face her. Instead he stayed with the palm of one hand flat against the panel, his arm locked at the elbow, staring straight ahead as if he couldn't maintain control of himself if he looked at her.

And Clair knew then that the man was just plain mad.

It was there in his ramrod-stiff spine, in the tightness of his jaw, even in the muscles and tendons that bulged in that arm stretched out to the door.

"We need to talk," Clair said, trying not to think about how imposing a sight was the enraged Ben.

"Uh-huh," he agreed, clearly keeping a tight rein on his temper. "But right now Reid doesn't want you upset. He wants you calm. So let's not."

"I want to. I'm not upset."

"Anymore? Because you were upset this morning. That's when all this started, remember?"

He still hadn't moved. He still wouldn't look at her.

"I'm not upset," she repeated, wondering if tension was the same thing but trying to hide that she was full of that.

"See, I'll even sit down," she said, perching on the couch at an angle that allowed her to continue to watch him. "But I need to talk about this. Please."

He sighed and she saw his jaw clench even tighter. But then he turned from the door and leaned his back against it instead. Crossing his arms over his chest, he finally looked at her.

But that hardly made her feel better. His eyes were stone-cold and his handsome face was so void of expression it was unnerving in itself.

"Okay," he conceded.

But he didn't say more than that, as if he still wasn't willing to discuss anything but was only humoring her.

"I'm sorry," Clair said then, plunging in. "I'm sorry for everything—beginning with the morning after the reunion and everything since."

He cocked his head slightly and when he responded to that his voice was quiet but gruff. "You're sorry for everything? For coming to Northbridge? Spending this time with me? Sleeping with me again? Letting me find out you're pregnant? Is that everything?"

"No, that's not the *everything* I'm talking about. I'm not sorry for coming to Northbridge or spending time with you or sleeping with you again. I am sorry that you found out about the baby the way you did, but not that you found out."

"Really? Because this morning you said you didn't know if you were going to tell me at all."

"I know. And I wasn't but—"

"You weren't sure if you were going to tell me, or you just weren't going to tell me?"

"I still wasn't sure if I was going to tell you," she confessed. And even though that was the lesser of the two evils she knew it sounded bad. "Please, Ben, I need you to understand—"

"I keep thinking what if this hadn't happened and you'd just left today? What if you'd left and never come back, never called, never let me know I was going to be—or *was*—a father? What if, twenty years from now a grown man knocked on my door and told me he was my son? Do you have any idea what that would have done to me? I grew up without a dad. And you could have caused my son—or daughter—to grow up without one, too."

"I didn't think about it that way," she confessed because it was true.

"What *did* you think about, Clair?"

"I know it will seem petty and small and selfish—and it was, it was backlash from my divorce and I just didn't know it until Cassie pointed it out to me at the hospital a little while ago. But even though I knew you had the right to know about the baby, to be a part of its life, to me it was…I just kept thinking that if you knew about the baby, if you had rights to it, it would be something you could take away from me."

"Like golden boy took things away from you," Ben said, shaking his head. "But this is a big deal, Clair. This isn't losing half the silverware. This isn't goldfish you replaced. This is a *child. My* child."

"I know. And you're probably thinking that it's as bad as what happened to you with that Heather person—"

"I'm thinking that I've made my life's work to help other people's kids, a lot of whom came from single-parent households or never knew who their parents were or whose problems stemmed from things their parents did—or didn't—do, and that I could have had a kid of my own out there who might have felt abandoned or neglected or cheated because they didn't have a dad."

Again, Clair hadn't thought of it that way. "I'm sorry.

I'm so, so sorry. All of that might have occurred to me in time and I'm not saying I was definitely, never, going to tell you about the baby. I've just been confused and worried and…I told you before, since the divorce I've felt as if I have to protect myself, and anything that's mine. And after having to go to war with Rob over every little thing, after losing things to him that I know he didn't even want just so he could strike some kind of blow against me, all I could think was that if this were Rob's baby, he would do whatever he could to take it from me, too."

"But I'm not Rob," Ben said slowly, pointedly.

"I know. Believe me, I know. I have sorted through that and I realized that you really wouldn't do anything to hurt me, to hurt the baby. That I was just looking at everything—at you—through some kind of thick divorce-fog. And I'm sorry for that. I'm really, really sorry."

Ben was staring at her very intently now, nodding his head knowingly, and although she could tell he retained some remnants of anger, it was dissipating.

"Okay," he said after a moment. "So that's the past. But here we are. And you're pregnant."

Clair mimicked his nod.

"Are you happy about it?" he asked.

"Shocked. But happy." And curious about his feelings, too. She just wasn't sure if she should ask.

"It rates high on the shock meter," he admitted, his brows arching for a moment in a forlorn frown.

"I'm sorry," she said yet again. "Of all the ways for you to find out—"

"Yeah, I don't think it's a story we'll want to tell the grandkids."

She wasn't sure how seriously he meant that but it gave her the first glimmer of hope that things between them might work out after all.

And that allowed her the courage to ask the question she hadn't moments before.

"What about you? Do you hate the idea of a baby?" she asked quietly.

"It's still sinking in, but no, I don't hate the idea, just the thought that I might never have known about it."

"But now you do."

"And now I'm wondering where this leaves us since you flipped out this morning over what I was proposing."

Proposing? Had he been proposing?

"You scared me," she told him.

"Yeah, I've always heard it can be pretty scary for someone to tell you they want you to stick around," he said sarcastically.

"It wasn't the sticking around part. It was the fact that it sounded good and that made me realize that you'd gotten closer than I thought you had, that I was more vulnerable to you—more vulnerable than I'd been to Rob. All of a sudden I just had so much at stake."

"Or not," he said, for the first time sounding like himself again. "There is another possibility in all this, you know. What I started to say this morning before you freaked was that I love you, Clair. That I want you in my life. That means we could get married, have this baby together, be a family, and neither of us would lose anything—we'd both just gain."

"*Was* that what you were going to say this morning? Before you knew about the baby?" she asked.

"What did you think I was saying?"

"It was kind of ambiguous. You could have been saying you wanted me to move back to Northbridge so we could date."

He grinned and Clair knew the worst was over. "To date," he repeated. "You thought I wanted you to uproot your whole life so we could be together—the way we were last night only long-term—just to *date?*"

"There was not really a *proposal* in it," she pointed out.

"I was working up to saying the actual words."

"Or maybe you're only saying the actual words now that there's a baby and you think you *have* to marry me."

He pushed away from the door with his shoulders and came to sit on the coffee table directly in front of her, taking her hands in his. "I do *have* to marry you but not because of the baby. I *have* to marry you because I'm in love with you. I *have* to marry you because I want you more than I've ever wanted anyone in my life. I *have* to marry you because I *have* to have you."

"You're sure?"

"Positive," he said convincingly. "Now tell me I haven't just been your rebound guy and that you'll marry me."

That made Clair laugh. "I did some thinking about that—about whether or not you were just rebound boy."

"And what did you decide?"

"I decided that when I'm with you it isn't my ego you're boosting. It's more along the lines of my libido."

He grinned again but this time it was that wicked grin of his. "Isn't that what got us into trouble this morning? I believe the way the nurse-midwife put it was *overly vigorous intercourse.* And imagine how funny my brother thought that was and how much it thrilled me to talk about it with the woman who taught my second grade health class."

"I wasn't too excited to know Cassie had overheard it, either."

"But I *do* excite you," Ben said with more of the devil in his tone.

"I think at this point that goes without saying," Clair said.

"You better marry me, then, or I'm cutting you off."

"Oh, well, in that case…" she joked.

Ben's expression grew serious again. "No, tell me for real," he urged solemnly.

"That I'll marry you?"

He confirmed that with a slight tilt of his chin.

"I will marry you. And not on the rebound and not because I *have* to. I love you, too. So much that that's actually what scared me. Too much *not* to scare me."

His eyes delved into hers. "You scared me pretty good today yourself," he confided then.

"When I told you I was pregnant?"

"When you told me something was wrong. When I saw for myself that you were scared-sick. Waiting at the hospital."

"But now everything has worked out," she reminded.

His somberness evolved into another smile. "Except that we can't consummate our engagement—vigorously or otherwise. At least for a few days."

"We'll just have to make up for it later," she said.

"That doesn't mean I can't kiss you, though," he warned a moment before he leaned forward, taking her mouth with his and pressing her to lie on the sofa so he could join her there.

He kissed her sweetly, conservatively, at first, obviously restraining himself.

And that was the way Clair responded. At first.

But the restraint they both started out with couldn't be maintained. Not when that kiss deepened. When lips parted. When tongues began to tease, to dart back and forth, to thrust in and out.

Certainly there was no restraint in Ben's repositioning himself so he was atop her. No restraint in his strong hand finding her breast—even if he did begin there, too, with caution and care and exquisite tenderness.

But before long the scant tank top she'd put on in such a hurry to go to the hospital had ridden upward and so had Ben's hand—underneath it rather than on top of it—finding her bare breast with the raw, sensual nakedness of that partially callused palm. Finding her taut nipple with talented fingers that traced circles, that trailed feathery tips to the very crest, that tugged and tormented and tortured her deliciously.

Certainly there was no restraint in Clair interrupting the play of mouths to pull off Ben's T-shirt. No restraint in letting her hands travel every inch of his back and then slide down to his perfect derriere to pull him against her, to feel the nudge of that long, hard ridge in front that let her know he honestly did want her. As much as she wanted him.

It was only when heartbeats were pounding and breathing was growing rapid and desire was rising to more demanding heights that Ben regained some restraint. Enough to stop kissing her, then start again, then stop and pull his hand out from under her tank top at the same time.

"A few days is going to seem like decades, isn't it?" he said in a gravely voice.

"Hey, I didn't start this, you did," Clair reminded, but her own voice was deeper and more sensuous than it had been earlier.

Ben pulsed his lower half against hers and said, "I'll finish it, too, as soon as I get the go-ahead."

Clair just smiled, taking that as a promise.

Then he rolled from on top of her to lie between her and the back of the couch, insinuating himself there until he was lying on his back and she was on her side, held close to him, her head on his chest, one thigh over his as his arms wrapped around her to hold her tight.

"I love you, Clair," he whispered into her hair.

"I love you, too," she whispered back.

Still holding her with one arm, he loosened the other so that he could lay a hand to her stomach. "We're going to have a *baby?*" he asked as if she'd just told him.

"Why yes, that's what I hear."

"So there, golden boy," he taunted.

Clair laughed and felt herself truly relax suddenly, enough to allow herself the full joy of that moment, of that man, of the fact that they'd actually created life together.

A life that she'd considered a gift even before then.

But as she lay there in his arms, it struck her that that life they'd created wasn't the only gift she'd been given at the class reunion. That Ben and the future—the long, forever-kind of storybook future that she felt sure they would have—made it a complete and wonderful package.

A complete and wonderful package that was worth every bit of the pain that had led her into Ben's arms that night in June.

* * * * *

Next month, look for
TALES FROM ELK CREEK,
two complete novels in one special volume,
part of Victoria Pade's
A RANCHING FAMILY miniseries.
Then, in March 2005, don't miss
HER SISTER'S KEEPER,
a brand-new, longer-length tale,
also part of her popular miniseries.

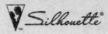

SPECIAL EDITION™

This month, Silhouette Special Edition
brings you the newest
Montana Mavericks story

ALL HE EVER WANTED

(SE #1664)

by reader favorite

Allison Leigh

When young Erik Stevenson fell down an abandoned
mine shaft, he was lucky to be saved by a brave—and
beautiful—rescue worker, Faith Taylor. She was struck by
the feelings that Erik's handsome father, Cameron, awoke
in her scarred heart and soul. But Cameron's heart had
barely recovered from the shock of losing his wife some
time ago. Would he be able to put the past aside—and
find happiness with Faith in his future?

GOLD RUSH GROOMS

Lucky in love—and striking it rich—
beneath the big skies of Montana!

**Don't miss this emotional story—
only from Silhouette Books.**

Available at your favorite retail outlet.

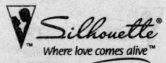

Where love comes alive™

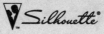

SPECIAL EDITION™

Don't miss a brand-new miniseries
coming to Silhouette Special Edition

THE
F**O**RTUNES
OF **TEXAS:**
Reunion

HER GOOD FORTUNE
by Marie Ferrarella

Available February 2005
Silhouette Special Edition #1665

Gloria Mendoza had returned to Texas for a
fresh start, and was determined not to get involved
with men. But when bank heir Jack Fortune was
assigned to help with her business affairs and
passion ignited between them, she realized some
vows were meant to be broken....

Fortunes of Texas: Reunion—
The power of family.

Available at your favorite retail outlet.

Where love comes alive™

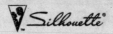

If you enjoyed what you just read,
then we've got an offer you can't resist!

Take 2 bestselling
love stories FREE!

Plus get a FREE surprise gift!

Clip this page and mail it to Silhouette Reader Service™

IN U.S.A.	**IN CANADA**
3010 Walden Ave.	P.O. Box 609
P.O. Box 1867	Fort Erie, Ontario
Buffalo, N.Y. 14240-1867	L2A 5X3

YES! Please send me 2 free Silhouette Special Edition® novels and my free surprise gift. After receiving them, if I don't wish to receive anymore, I can return the shipping statement marked cancel. If I don't cancel, I will receive 6 brand-new novels every month, before they're available in stores! In the U.S.A., bill me at the bargain price of $4.24 plus 25¢ shipping and handling per book and applicable sales tax, if any*. In Canada, bill me at the bargain price of $4.99 plus 25¢ shipping and handling per book and applicable taxes**. That's the complete price and a savings of at least 10% off the cover prices—what a great deal! I understand that accepting the 2 free books and gift places me under no obligation ever to buy any books. I can always return a shipment and cancel at any time. Even if I never buy another book from Silhouette, the 2 free books and gift are mine to keep forever.

235 SDN DZ9D
335 SDN DZ9E

Name	(PLEASE PRINT)	
Address	Apt.#	
City	State/Prov.	Zip/Postal Code

Not valid to current Silhouette Special Edition® subscribers.

Want to try two free books from another series?
Call 1-800-873-8635 or visit www.morefreebooks.com.

* Terms and prices subject to change without notice. Sales tax applicable in N.Y.
** Canadian residents will be charged applicable provincial taxes and GST.
All orders subject to approval. Offer limited to one per household.
® are registered trademarks owned and used by the trademark owner and or its licensee.

SPED04R   ©2004 Harlequin Enterprises Limited